Kath
Sister of
my heart, Love

# Telling
# Sky

by Kris Owen

**DORRANCE**
PUBLISHING CO
EST. 1920
PITTSBURGH, PENNSYLVANIA 15238

Dorrance Publishing Co
585 Alpha Drive
Pittsburgh, PA 15238
Visit our website at *www.dorrancebookstore.com*

ISBN: 978-1- 4809-5633- 9
eISBN: 978-1- 4809-5610- 0

As she pushed through the trees and brush, she felt her sandals fall off. The earth and grass felt cool between her toes. There was no stopping now. She wasn't out of breath. Her pace was more of a hurried walk than a run. Here she felt light and giggly like a child. The smell of damp earth mixed with pine, balsam, and juniper were fragrances she knew well. This was home, where her heart was light and her spirit could be free.

The June sky was pastel blue with white, wispy clouds that brushed the sun as if playing tag. Her body felt pleasantly warm. A cool breeze dipped across the mountains, keeping the air light and comfortable on this beautiful, early summer day. As the bank of the river appeared before her, she slowed her pace. Delighting her eyes, the crystal-clear water revealed sculptured sand and an assortment of glistening rocks that the rapidly moving water masterfully offered to nature.

Her dreams brought her back to this place again and again, but this time was different. This was no dream. Here, she felt young and filled with all the possibilities of life, especially today.

Leaning against a large outcropping of rock, she paused to soak in the moment. Anna ran away from life today. It was just for today, but, nevertheless, she had escaped from her usual, ordinary day. She smiled to herself enjoying her success. No one knew she had stolen the day and that made it hers alone.

The silence was broken by the swish of leaves moving in the breeze as Sedge Wrens busily flew about the riverbank. She pulled her jacket tight, feeling as if she were giving herself a hug. A baby, she thought, my baby - mine and Aaron's baby. Life was all mixed up, but the thought of having Aaron's baby made Anna happy - happier than she had been in a long time. Right now, it was all she knew for sure.

Sleep never came easily to Anna, but as of late, it was fitful, and she often awoke exhausted. Her dreams were vivid and aroused a feeling of sadness in her. The dreams came as visions with moving colors and distorted shapes. Awaking often, she felt tense and uneasy. This morning she opened her eyes with a start; her heart racing and her breath rapid. Pulling the sheets to her chest, she glanced over at the empty space that once cradled her husband, Aaron. Reaching out, she imagined brushing his back softly with her fingertips as she had done so often. The memory of the sweet smell of his skin relaxed her. Moving over, her naked body settled into his side of the bed, and she felt safe.

The alarm sounded, and Anna began her day. A three-mile run was her usual morning practice; then a quick shower, a power drink, and a cup of coffee to go. She smiled remembering: this was their ritual before the accident.

Before leaving for work, Aaron would kiss Anna lightly on the cheek and head out. Anna watched him from the kitchen window as he drove down the driveway to the street. He looked handsome in his National Forest uniform. Even though he was 45, his strong build, square jaw, and full head of dark hair gave him a youthful appearance and made him very good to look at. Aaron was fit and was dedicated to staying that way. Anna was attracted to him the first time their eyes met, so many years before.

*　　*　　*　　*　　*

Anna didn't have to go into the office today. Her job as a reporter for the local newspaper allowed her to work from home most days. Her schedule was unpredictable, but she managed her time so she could cover local community events. Weekends were filled with photo ops and human-interest stories, which were her favorite. The newspaper editor, Terri, covered the politics of the area. John, the sports editor, covered school events, NASCAR, and the area's track and field schedule. Helen, the administrative assistant, managed the clerical tasks and kept everyone informed about upcoming events, new business openings, the current status of advertising dollars and, of great importance, the circulation numbers.

The Reporter covered news and community events for twenty-one towns in the White Mountains of New Hampshire. Anna enjoyed telling the stories of the neighborhoods, and she was pleasantly surprised when her unexpected natural talent for photography brought acclaim. She had the ability to tell a story in both written word and photograph.

Anna and Aaron's family consisted of Bud, a twelve-year-old, black Lab, Max, a six-year-old golden, and, Cayenne, a three-year-old cockapoo. They were their children, and they referred to them as their boys. Anna, now 40, resigned herself to being mommy to her furry babies. Aaron and she stopped talking about the family they might one day have years before. As time passed, their focus changed and life was full.

Anna replayed the events of the fateful day. Only two months had passed since life changed so dramatically. She tried to put the pieces together, replaying the scene in her mind again and again; imagining Aaron driving up the dirt, mountain road just as he had so many times before, safely.

Aaron's job was a perfect fit. He loved the White Mountains and their history. When he was a boy, he hiked and fished many of the places he eventually patrolled as a forest ranger and now managed as the forest supervisor. Being outdoors in nature was as natural to him as breathing.

Growing up on his family's farm in the White Mountains wasn't easy. Aaron often spoke of Grandfather Knox, who was the man of the house when Aaron grew up. His grandfather lived life by the strength of his word and the good book.

If Aaron delayed carrying out a chore, his grandfather would say, "Working the land grows a body," assuring him that he still had a lot of growing to do.

Chores were to be done in a very specific way, and a close inspection made by his grandfather insured it would be done right, no matter how many times it had to be done.

Aaron and his family were the fourth generation to work the farm. His heritage included a strong reverence for the land and the soil that gives birth to the crops. The animals that provided food and comfort were given great care and, sometimes funny names.

In a small cemetery at the bottom of the hill, beloved family members were set to rest. The sacred earth was decorated with handcrafted headstones that reflected a brief story of their life. All of it, combined with his grandfather's strong, occasionally gnarly, but always loving direction, guided Aaron's young life.

*   *   *   *   *

Grandfather Knox stepped in when Aaron's father walked out on the family. Only once did Aaron hear his grandfather speak of his father.

He simply said, "Your father didn't have the back for long workdays, or the strength of character needed to take care of his family, the animals, and the fields. He was a spoiled, city boy. You and your mother are better off without him."

Aaron's mother, Sky, and his father, Josh, met through friends, fell in love, and married, after knowing each other for only two months. The small cottage just behind the Knox farmhouse, with a few repairs made by Grandfather Knox, made a perfect home for the newlyweds.

Aaron's father, an only child, grew up in an affluent household in Boston and wanted for very little. He was a handsome, charming man who had difficulty keeping a job. With little to no income, Josh was expected to work the land alongside Grandfather Knox, but the grueling farm life demanded more than he was able or willing to give.

By the time Aaron was born, the strain on the marriage was evident. The first time Aaron's dad held him was the day he was brought home from the hospital. Sky spoke lovingly of how tiny he looked in his father's arms, and how her heart was filled with joy as she watched the love of her life rock their infant son to sleep. He then placed Aaron gently into his cradle, and kissed him on the forehead. The next morning his father was gone.

There was no communication between his mother and father after that day. His grandfather and mother were his family. He wondered occasionally what his life would have been like if his father hadn't left, but he didn't miss the father he never got to know.

When Aaron was fifteen, his mother received a phone call and learned her husband and the father of her child died in a car accident in New York City. She was told by Josh's family that he was being buried over the weekend, but there was no need for her to attend. They made it clear that they did not consider them to be part of the family.

The only memories Aaron had of his father were the stories he was told by his mother and a few words said by his grandfather. In the bottom drawer of his bedroom bureau he stored two pictures: one taken on the day his mother and father were married and one of his father holding him in his arms. The picture was taken as he sat in the rocker on the day Aaron came home from the hospital. The photos were worn, black and white snapshots, but the only connection he ever had to his father.

According to Grandfather Knox, Aaron's mother fell into a deep depression after her husband left. She struggled to care for her new son, but was consumed with mourning for her lost love and longing for him to return. Even though she was aware of her husband's discontent, she believed he would learn to revere the land as she did.

Grandfather Knox guided Aaron through life's challenges, doing what he could to cover for his emotionally absent mother and make up for the father that had abandon him. Aaron loved his grandfather and followed his example closely. As the years passed Aaron grew into a strong, gentle, funny man, making his mother and grandfather proud. Grandfather Knox was steadfast in his quest to fill the void left by Aaron's dad.

Although Aaron's mother fought chronic depression, she functioned as best she could. Only Aaron could make her smile. Most days she dressed, ate whatever Grandfather Knox prepared, and sat in her rocking chair on the front porch, waiting for her husband to return.

*　　　*　　　*　　　*　　　*

Grandfather Knox lived a long, but not unchallenging, life. Not a stranger to loss, his deep, abiding faith sustained him. He taught Aaron to be honest and to stand up for what he believed in. Respect for his fellow man was essential to him as was his unwavering reverence for the land and all things created by God. Aaron had great respect for the man who shaped his young life with strength and love, and wanted to be just like him.

When Aaron was a boy his grandfather told him tales of his ancestors, the Pennacook Indian tribe, who settled in the White Mountains long ago. He spoke of their customs and spiritual beliefs. Grandfather Knox was a proud descendant of the Pennacook Tribe. Aaron's keen respect for nature was an outgrowth of the Knox family character and became the fabric of his life from a very early age.

Grandfather often told stories of the tribe's struggle with infectious diseases that were carried by the newcomers who settled in the area. The tribe grew ill and weak, and was subject to raids by the Mohawk. He saw the Knox farmland and the surrounding wooded area as a symbol of his ancestors who walked the land before them. It was a testament to the days when the tribe was strong and independent.

Loosely translated, Pennacook means "at the bottom of the hill." Grandfather honed his grave marker many years before he died, placing it where he would be laid to rest in the little cemetery at the bottom of the hill.

Aaron listened intently as his grandfather described what the Indians call a Vision Quest. He imagined himself a young Indian boy readying to enter manhood. Grandfather Knox spoke of the Indian folklore that was wrapped in symbolism. He spoke in simple terms, explaining that the purpose of the Quest was to provide a young man with a deep understanding of his life's purpose. A young brave would trek into the woods with only the bare necessities for survival, while fasting. There he would stay until his spirit animal appeared to him.

Aaron was captivated each time his grandfather eloquently wove the tail of his own journey into manhood, painting a magical picture of his experience. The totem animal that came to him was the wolf. His totem symbolically represented stamina and the teacher. The close-knit packs provided the wolf with a strong sense of family, traits Grandfather Knox honored his whole life.

Grandfather also told another story that Aaron loved to hear. He had a vision just before Aaron was born. A wolf appeared one morning just before sunrise as he was plowing a field. The wolf moved slowly, cautiously, to the middle of the row that was being readied for planting. Following close behind was her cub. Grandfather stopped the plow allowing the mother and cub to pass. The air was unusually still, and the penetrating stare of the mother wolf left him in awe.

Grandfather Knox honored the symbolism of the wolf throughout his life. He understood at that moment in the field, that he would be responsible for the protection of the new life about to be born. The wolf foretold that he would be needed as a loving guide, always watchful, as his grandchild moved across the sometimes-arduous fields of life.

*    *    *    *    *

Grandfather Knox lost Edna, his first wife, suddenly. Aaron only knew what his mother told him of his grandmother's death. His grandfather never spoke of it.

His mother reverently relived the day she lost her mother. After a long afternoon working in the fields, her father came home for the evening meal as he usually did. Tired and hungry, he could tell dinner was ready by the smell of home cooking that lingered in the air as he climbed the front porch stairs. Taking his boots off outside before entering, as he always did, he noticed the house was eerily quiet. His senses immediately told him something was wrong. Sky and her brother, Tayac, were still outside playing in the backyard, which was unusual for that time of day. He called out. The pots on the stove were steaming, and the table was set for the evening meal, but Edna was nowhere to be seen.

Calling her name, he walked toward the bedroom. The door was slightly ajar. Moving closer, he pushed the door, opening it wide. His senses rose to high alert when saw his wife lying on the floor, motionless. Calling her name, he ran to her side. Lifting her, he placed her limp body gently on the bed and tucked a pillow beneath her head. She was not breathing; there was no movement - no response of any kind. Edna looked like she was sleeping, but in his heart, he knew she was gone.

It took hours for the country doctor to arrive at the Knox farm and confirm what the family already knew. He called it an aneurysm and said she went quickly.

The children were fed and bedded by a woman from a farm up the road. She cried with them, hugged them tight, and tucked them in. When they were asleep, she went about the task of washing and dressing Edna, readying her for burial the next morning.

Grandfather Knox placed his sorrow in the task at hand, working in the barn, honing the simple, wooden casket that would hold his beloved wife's remains until the end of time. In the morning, a modest, mule-drawn wagon hauled it to the family cemetery. Family and friends gathered around the gravesite for the simple ceremony. After, the men went back to the fields and the women tended to the children. Brokenhearted, the following day Sky and Tayac returned to their little, one room schoolhouse.

*     *     *     *     *

Grandfather was left to raise his seven-year-old daughter and four-year-old son alone. Her mother's death left Sky, an already sensitive child, reeling in fear and anxiety. She struggled to understand why God would take her mother away. Her father, steeped in anger and sadness from the loss of his wife, didn't know how to comfort his children. He only knew how to keep them safe and fed. All of his strength went into the land, the only thing he understood.

Sky thought her father was angry with her, afraid she was somehow responsible for her mother's death. Her father didn't offer tender words, nor did he have an explanation of why bad things sometime happen.

On the day their mother died, he held his children close, wrapping his arms around them, jaw rigid and fists clinched tightly. He had no words of comfort to offer them. Edna was buried in the cemetery at the bottom of the hill with all the family members that left before her. After the ceremony Edna's name was never again spoken. Local church women stepped in to help the family and nurture the motherless children, but their father, struggling with anger, remained emotionally absent.

As was the community's practice, an alternating schedule of volunteers stepped up to help the family through their sudden loss and difficult mourning period. On weekends a woman from a nearby farm would prepare a meal and round up her children to visit the Knox household for the afternoon. It was the only meal Sky and Tayac shared with a family. During the week meals were dropped off by neighbors. It was Sky's job to warm them in the oven and encourage Tayac to eat. During the week the children ate alone, did their homework as the sun went down, and waited for their father to come in from the fields. When he did, he ate and readied for bed. He listened to their prayers, tucked them in, and kissed them on the forehead. There was little conversation and little joy.

*     *     *     *     *

One year after Edna's death, tragedy struck again. Sky's younger brother, Tayac, lost his life in a tragic accident. The children were playing hide and seek as they often did on a bright, sunny, afternoon. River water, high from the spring thaw, rushed quickly downstream. Rumbling in the distance was the sound of the wagon as their father moved bales of hay. The lunch bell rang as Mrs. Maroney, a woman from a neighboring farm, called them to lunch.

Tayac heard the bell. Jumping onto the nearest rock to make his way home, his foot hit a patch of wet moss causing him to lose his balance. The soft, sand-like earth gave away beneath his feet. Grabbing frantically onto a branch of a nearby tree, desperate to stop his fall, his weight separated the dead limb from the trunk. Hanging on to the branch, he tumbled down the embankment into the turbulent river.

Sky heard his cries and ran toward the river to help. All she could see was the top of Tayac's head as the rapidly moving water swept him down the river. She ran into the field screaming frantically searching for her father. Hearing the panic in his daughter's voice, he immediately knew that something was wrong.

Sky, moving as quickly as her legs would carry her, led her father to the edge of the river where she last saw her brother. The unstable white water swept downed branches and swirling leaves past them, but there was no sign of Tayac as far as they could see.

Crying, Sky ran along the bank. "Right there, he was right there! I saw him right there!"

Later that afternoon, volunteers, praying that the young boy they were searching for was safe, found Tayac's lifeless body. He was floating peacefully in a riverside wetland surrounded by yellow Water Lilies. A large boulder ended his journey downstream, rocking him gently until he was claimed by his loved ones.

*    *    *    *    *

The sudden death of Sky's brother only a year after the death of her mother left the eight-year-old in an even greater emotional abyss. As the years passed neither she nor her father could come to terms with the tragic losses they suffered. Sky's father survived by immersing himself in his work. Sky attended church and bible school, but was unable to connect to the God that took her mother and brother away. She was surviving, but felt empty and useless. Sky was haunted by the feeling that she was somehow responsible for the death of her mother and her brother.

*    *    *    *    *

Seven years after Edna's death, Sky's father remarried. The marriage was arranged and took place after the crops were harvested. His new wife, Betsy, had a dowry that included two acres of fertile pasture and two foals.

After her mother's death Sky took over the household chores as best she could. As she began to develop, as young girls do, it was apparent to her father that Sky needed a woman in her life. On an early fall morning, he walked several miles up the road to the Williams farm and asked old man Williams for his daughter's hand in marriage. Knox expected her to cook, clean, attend to all wifely duties, as well as instruct Sky on how to become a good wife.

Betsy was fifteen years Knox's junior and seven years older than Sky. At twenty-one she had never had a suitor. Her father, worried about her future, considered marriage to a farmer the only way for his daughter to have a good life. They agreed on the union and the dowry with a handshake.

It was a quick ceremony on a sunny, Sunday afternoon that brought the unlikely pair together as husband and wife. There was no celebration. Betsy was what Knox needed to help raise his daughter and allow him to keep up with the ever-changing needs of the land. She was the oldest girl of a large family who began helping her mother in the kitchen from a young age. In addition, she was well versed in canning and the art of needlecraft.

After the wedding Betsy moved her meager belongings into the big bedroom at the top of the stairs. She was a hard worker and, from the beginning, labored beside her husband in the fields when needed. When not in the fields her time was filled with cooking, cleaning, and helping her stepdaughter with homework. She was there to answer Sky's questions about her blooming womanhood and teach her all she needed to know about becoming a good wife.

Betsy was a large-framed woman with jet black hair that she pulled back into a braid. Each morning before breakfast she tightly crafted a thick, waist length weave that cascaded into a fine point fastened by a rubber band. By evening long strands of hair floated free behind her, bobbing to and fro as she moved. In the kitchen, and when working in the fields, she wore a long, white apron over an ankle length, navy blue, cotton dress. The apron tied neatly around her waist and was held tightly in place by a big, floppy bow. Two large square pockets on the front served as a storage place for a wooden spoon or two, and matchsticks that peeked from the opening. Betsy could be heard humming in the kitchen as she busily made meals for her new husband and stepdaughter.

After the wedding Sky's father came home for dinner every evening and they ate together as a family. Tayac's chair remained in place, painfully vacant. There was always polite conversation and dessert. Sky ate, said little, and helped with clean up. When the kitchen was in order Betsy sat at the table and reviewed Sky's homework. The truth was, Betsy had only gone to the fourth grade. She was taken out of school to help out at home as more babies were born. Her homework duties were a façade at best, but no one seemed to be the wiser.

Sky was a serious teenager who did what was asked of her, but seldom smiled. She ached for her mother's arms around her and missed her little brother's teasing and prodding. She woke nights crying as her dreams brought her images of Tayac being stolen by the river current.

It was inappropriate for Sky to call her new mother Betsy, but she couldn't bring herself to call her mother. After several months of awkward conversation, in a moment of frustration, Sky called Betsy Mamma, and from that time on Mamma was her name.

At times Sky pretended she was her mother. Mamma did her best to nurture and protect her, but Mamma could never replace the deep, nurturing love Sky lost when her mother died.

\*　　\*　　\*　　\*　　\*

Aaron remembered when his mother told him that Mamma was diagnosed with cancer. He was just a teenager, but watched in awe as his rough and tumble grandfather gently dressed his wife, fed her, and tended to her needs. A remarkable, but sullen man, he cared for his dying wife, attended to the demands of the farm, and watched over his fragile daughter, all while supporting the needs of his growing grandson. The long hours and unrelenting demands of the fields were part of his day, every day.

After fighting years of a losing battle, Mamma slipped away. The little cemetery in the pine grove at the bottom of the hill was the resting place for another Knox family member.

\*　　\*　　\*　　\*　　\*

Aaron's mother revered the American Indian traditions that were part of her family history. She, too, enjoyed listening to stories of the culture, traditions and strong beliefs of the Pennacook people. Sky was a beautiful, but fretful baby and, when she was happy, it was as if the sun came out from behind the clouds. When she lost her mother and her brother, her days were mostly stormy.

Sky grew into an attractive woman with a small frame, thick, black, wavy hair and dark brown eyes that flashed with the sunlight. Her bright, lively eyes grew dull when life's struggles grew more than she could bear. When her husband left her and their newborn son she again ascended into a life filled with cloudy days. Even as a little boy, Aaron knew his mother's sadness depleted her energy. For many years the love of her son and the enduring presences of her father were the only things in her life that she felt connected to.

\*　　\*　　\*　　\*　　\*

At the age of 70, Grandfather Knox died suddenly of a heart attack while working the field. When he didn't return home for the evening meal, Aaron went looking for him. He found him lying beside a wagon piled high with bales of hay. Aaron lifted him, carried him back to the house, and laid him down on his bed.

His death was the end of an era. Tears were shed and, once again, the community gathered to put another Knox family member to rest. The grave marker Grandfather Knox chiseled long ago simply said, "Love of Family, the Earth, and the Kingdom of God guided this imperfect soul all the days of his life."

*  *  *  *  *

The house that had been the center of many generations of family, was now quiet and seemed empty. Sky's father was her rock, the strength she needed to navigate life's storms. His loss and Aaron's nearing departure for college left her feeling alone and isolated. The responsibility of the farm now fell on her shoulders alone; shoulders that had always been frail. Aaron helped out when he could, but his life course was moving in another direction. He was headed to college and, more than anything else, he wanted to be a forest ranger. Aaron knew it was the first time his mother would have the responsibility of running the farm without her father's wisdom and guidance.

Holding his mother's hand, he said what he believed his grandfather would have wanted. "Mom, I'm going to put off going to college for a while. You need me here, and I need to be here for you."

Sky's eyes filled with tears. Closing them, she took a deep breath and bowed her head.

As she spoke, she placed her hand over her heart. "No, Aaron, this time belongs to you. Go where life is leading you. College is your destination right now. I'll hire a foreman to help me with the land and do the best I can to keep the farm going. I'm not your grandfather, but I do have his blood in me. I'll do the best I can, and time will tell if it's good enough."

The day of her father's funeral Sky was sullen and moved mechanically through the quiet ceremony and burial. Her father's plain, wooden coffin was lowered into the ground as the fall wind curved the treetops toward the earth as if they were mourning his loss.

*    *    *    *    *

The pain of loss was a frequent visitor in Sky's life. The night of her father's ceremony was but another grief filled evening. It was quiet, the guests were gone, and Aaron was in bed asleep. As she gazed into the evening sky, she felt comforted by the violet colored mountains. Praying was not something Sky usually did. Even when sitting in church she hadn't prayed for a long time.

This evening was different; Sky sat and waited – waiting for God to take away her pain. But, on this evening she whispered silently to heaven for help. For years Sky tried to make sense of death, but, in doing so, lost her connection to life. There were so many unanswered questions; why did God take her baby brother? Why did her mother have to die? Why did her husband leave her and their new born son? How could she live without her father to guide and care for her? What had she done to deserve all this pain? If there was a God, why did he take so many loved ones away from her? She felt alone and powerless.

The family farm was the only home she knew. Sky was born in the small, back bedroom of the farmhouse and, three years later, in the same bedroom her little brother, Tayac, was born. Both Sky and Tayac had been given Indian names by their father, a Knox family tradition. Life was simple. As they grew they worked the land and sold produce at market. The women canned and prepared for the long New Hampshire winters. Tayac rode the wagon with his father and helped feed the animals.

Sky's and Tayac's grandfather, the original homesteader, was a direct descendant of Passaconaway, Chief of the Pennacook Indian tribe. Their father often told them bedtime stories, weaving colorful tales of their grandfather's people and their magical, spiritual qualities.

Sky wondered about the spiritual beings of the stories he told. Where were they when her baby brother died? After his death, it was years before her pain dulled, her tears stopped, and laughter made its way back into her life. When her son, Aaron, was born it was like the sun came out again.

The night of her father's service, as she sat looking at the mountains, she took a long, deep breath. Sky remembered that it was her mother's deep belief in God that kept her strong through the storms of her life. Sky lost her faith somewhere amid her losses. To her, the mountains were symbolic of something else, something stronger than she was. Childhood stories flooded her memory. She recalled her mother's loving voice. Sky imagined her Indian ancestors dancing before her, calling on her to join them and a higher power in their dance.

Suddenly a bright, crescent shaped moon decorated the cool night sky, and she was surrounded by a stillness that she had never experienced before.

For the first time since her mother died, she spoke to the God of her childhood. "If you're up there, please give me a sign. I'm lost and don't know what to do. Please show me the way."

Softly laughing at herself and her need to believe as her mother had, she continued. "If I join my ancestors in the circle dance, will you join us, too, my God? Would you move the moon up and down in the sky I was named for, so I'll know you hear me?"

Sitting back on the large wooden rocker her father had made for her when Aaron was born, she wrapped her comforter around herself and pulled her knees up, crossing them in front of her Indian style. Sky had decisions to make and thought how much better it would be if she had the spirit guides of her father.

The window she was gazing from framed the mountains and the night sky, accenting the view as if it were an artist's canvas. Her wondering eyes opened wide in disbelief as the window view was flooded with light. The front field of the farmhouse grew brighter; slowly at first, then intensifying until Sky could see only a bright, white, glowing light. She moved her hand to her forehead to shade her eyes from the intensity of the rays. It couldn't possibly be the sun that was spreading the light across the evening sky. She held her breath and watched in wonder and disbelief. In minutes, it began to retreat until, once again, only the crescent shaped moon and starlight remained.

Sky questioned what she had just seen or had she just imagined.

Warm, salty tears rolled down her cheeks and slid into the corners of her mouth. An unexpected laugh rose from the center of her being. She accepted the fact that the sky lit up for her that night. There was no explanation, no witness, no proof, but she knew in her heart it was true. Sky asked for a sign, and it was given. It was not her imagination, and she was certain at last she was not alone.

"Thank you." Sky whispered, "I understand."

Life did not change magically for her after her vision; not the next day, the next week or year. The change was in her. She knew each day was meant to be lived on purpose, and she began each day with gratitude. Over time, the sadness that Sky had carried for so long lifted. She smiled often and laughed regularly.

\*     \*     \*     \*     \*

Home on school break, Aaron noticed the change in his mother. She was stronger and seemed happy for the first time. He watched in awe as she managed all the demands of the farm. It allowed him to go back to college knowing his mother was happy at last. She was finally at peace.

"Life is about change," she would say to Aaron. "Just as the fields change with the seasons, our lives change as well."

When Sky attended church each Sunday she joined in to pray and give thanks. After a time, she became a leader and confidant in the ladies groups and was sought out for her wisdom and carefully considered advice. For many years she just sat in the church pew wondering why God had forsaken her. Now Sky felt a presence, and it permeated her smile and everything she did. People were drawn to her warmth and gentleness. In addition to managing the farm, Sky became active in her church socials, helping out whenever she was needed. Her life was full. When she went to bed at night she slept soundly. The night sky, no matter what time of year, brought her peace and reminded her that she was never alone.

\*     \*     \*     \*     \*

A new season in Sky's life began one Sunday at church as she was collecting prayer books from the pews after the service. At the back of the church there stood a man she didn't recognize. He was tall, slim, looking to be about fifty, with slightly graying hair. As she glanced up from the neatly piled books, he smiled.

"May I help you?" she asked.

He nodded. "Yes, as a matter of fact. I understand there's a bereavement group that meets here on Sunday afternoons."

"Yes," she responded, still smiling. "The group meets at six o'clock. Will you be joining us?"

Looking slightly uncomfortable, he continued, "I will be. My friend recommended it. My wife passed away six months ago. I'm still trying to figure out how to live life without her."

"I understand," was all she could say.

That's how it began. It was unexpected. They got to know each other over the next year, sharing stories of their lost love and the challenge of coping with the pain that remained. One night after the group meeting, Don asked her to join him for coffee. Together they left the structure of the church support group and traveled into a relationship that bloomed from healing.

Aaron was happy that his mother found peace and love at last. Don and his mother married in the fall and settled into the farmhouse. Sky was sure the ancestors would approve.

*     *     *     *     *

The death of his grandfather triggered an inescapable mourning Aaron had never felt for his father, a void he didn't know how to fill. He missed his grandfather's strong presence. What Aaron knew for sure was that he was forever changed. Always at home in the White Mountains, the farm of his youth no longer fit his life.

When Aaron was fifteen, just after he received the news of his father's death, he readied for his Vision Quest. With his mother's permission, he relied on his grandfather's guidance to fulfill his mission. Grandfather Knox carefully instructed him. He had to fast for the duration of the Quest starting the day it began. While walking through the woods he was instructed to find a location that felt naturally comfortable, somehow familiar. There, he was to draw a ten-foot circle in which he would spend the next two to four days fasting, opening himself up to connect to the animal spirit that would guide him in his journey on earth.

He was told the spirit he was waiting for would come in the form of what Native Americans call an animal totem, and may appear in a vision or in physical form. The purpose of the animal totem's appearance was to deliver a message that would guide him in his life's course. If the animal showed up in physical form Aaron was to collect something that was connected to it; a feather, fur, or the earth on which it stood. Saving it would be a powerful reminder of the vision, and an indication that he intended to honor the message it represented, a symbol of wisdom and guidance.

Aaron was cautiously excited. He fasted as instructed and, early on a bright October morning, began his journey into the woods of New Hampshire to find sacred ground to draw his circle and wait for his spirit guide. In his backpack, he brought water and a blanket. His grandfather fashioned a walking stick for him and his mother gave him a journal. Aaron was the same age Grandfather Knox was when he ventured out on his Vision Quest.

Walking through the woods Aaron felt exhilarated. The sun streaming across the tree branches offered an arch overhead that glowed of crimson, gold, and orange foliage. He followed the fall rainbow of color hoping it would lead him to a place for his sacred circle. As he maneuvered through the woods, he was drawn to a large bolder that sat overlooking the Pemigewasset River. The day was cool, and the fallen leaves crunched under his feet as he moved forward, looking for a stretch of land that felt just right. Aaron wasn't sure how he knew when he came to it, but he did. He found the perfect place to draw his sacred circle.

As he fashioned the circle he imagined it as a fortress giving him a sense of safety. It was where he would spend the next couple of days. Next, he had to build a fire. The October evening temperature reminded him that he needed protection from the cold. Grandfather Knox taught him long ago how to create a fire out of dead leaves and tree branches. He rubbed dried sticks together and watched in satisfaction as sparks rose out of the billows of smoke and ignited the carefully arranged leaves and sticks. The small accomplishment made him feel more confident that he would be successful in his Quest. When the fire was strong he scouted for more leaves and sticks to feed his fire throughout the night.

From the position of the sun he calculated the time to be about noon. Ignoring his growling stomach, he systematically combed the area trying to recall everything Grandfather Knox taught him on their weekend camping trips.

"The trees are your friends," his grandfather would say. "They will protect and shelter you. Be mindful, they also protect and shelter the animals. Always respect the space you are walking in, it does not belong to you alone."

Aaron lay back using his backpack as a pillow. The wind released leaves into the air and he watched them float back and forth in the breeze as they traveled to earth. The scent of pine was strong, and he could hear the river water as it rushed from the mountains to the open arms of the ocean. His stomach grumbled, the fire crackled, and the heat from the flames warmed his face. He felt his body finally relax as he surrendered to sleep.

It was dark when Aaron woke with a start. The fire had almost burnt out, so he quickly moved to feed the flames. He was grateful he woke up. If the fire had gone out he would have been sleeping without the protection of the flame that staved off the woodland creatures, but he wondered what had awakened him. Sitting cross-legged close to the warmth of the fire, he scanned the area outside the circle. The sky was deep blue except for a patchwork of stars, but he could see nothing beyond the clusters of white birch, maple, and pine trees. He quieted himself for meditation and to gather peace.

Morning came delivering a light drizzle. Aaron fashioned an arch out of pine branches, moving under it to stay out of the rain. The grumbling in his stomach stopped, but he occasionally felt pangs of hunger. The scent of the damp earth was strong and made him think of fishing trips with his grandfather. He filled the day by watching the clouds float across the sky, finding animal shapes and funny faces looking back at him. Falling asleep in the afternoon, he was awakened late in the evening to a sound in the distance. Reaching out with a long branch he stoked the fire. Moving his knees against his chest he wondered what could be lurking in the woods. Aaron imagined his circle as a grand barrier and his fire as Mother Nature's warning to the woodland creatures to stay away. After a long vigil, he once again slipped into a deep sleep.

The third day was unusually warm for October, but Aaron welcomed the change. The fire still burned bright and collecting leaves and brush to keep it alive passed the time. He was beginning to think he wouldn't be blessed with the appearance of a totem animal. After all his time there, he had seen nothing but squirrels gathering acorns for the winter and some small birds flying in and out of the tree branches.

Again, Aaron napped, waking in the darkness of night. As he sat and listened, something felt different. Interrupting the stillness of the evening was the deep melodious, mating song of bullfrogs. He could hear the swish of tree branches as they swayed in the wind; clear and rhythmic. Everything around him seemed brighter; the colors, the smells, and the movement of the river water reverberated like a magnificent orchestra serenading him.

Scanning his sacred circle, he noticed movement in the direction of a bolder located on the far side of his circle. The dancing fire lit up the area. Standing on top of the bolder, looking in Aaron's direction, a small coyote stood motionless. Its fur was thick and rugged looking. The tips of its ears and front of its legs and paws were a mix of gray, black, and red. A streak of white fir swooped from his jaw to his underbelly and down the back of its legs. His tail was long and thick, moving back and forth in slow motion as he watched Aaron with laser focus. His eyes were gold, strangely reminding him of his grandfather.

A gust of wind moved leaves up and around in a connecting, circular dance. The moon's light accented the view as if nature was playing in the evening light. In seconds the coyote was gone.

Aaron was stunned and amazed. He walked toward the bolder where the coyote stood, listening intently as he approached. He questioned himself. Had the coyote actually been there or was it a vision, perhaps, created in his mind in a desire to connect with his totem animal? Aaron curled up, covered himself with a blanket of leaves, and drifted off to sleep. The vision of the coyote sitting on the bolder at the edge of his circle drifted in and out of his dreams.

Morning came bringing bright sunshine. Aaron knew it was time to go home. He walked one last time to the bolder and, to his delight, the morning light reveled a very distinct paw print left by the coyote. Scooping the rocks and earth that held the print, he filled his leather pouch. This was the proof he needed. The coyote had actually been there just as he recalled. He was sure now that it was his totem animal. Once he returned home Grandfather Knox would tell him the folklore connected to the coyote. His Vision Quest was a success, and he was proud.

Aaron headed home. The time he spent in the woods would be held in his memory for all time. He was feeling a little dizzy as he approached the back door of the farmhouse. It was very apparent that he needed to eat. When he entered the kitchen, his mother and grandfather were waiting for him. Food was the first thing on his mind. His mother had prepared his favorite breakfast, confident they would be celebrating his success. Aaron ate slowly, savoring every bite, and happy to be home.

When he cleaned his plate, Grandfather Knox was the first to speak. "Did you accomplish what you set out to do, son?"

Aaron smiled. "Yes, Grandfather. It was not what I expected, but I believe my animal totem is the coyote. One showed up the night before I left. He stood on the top of a nearby bolder overlooking my circle. As he stared into my eyes I felt like he knew me, and then he was gone as quickly as he appeared. I have the earth from where he stood in my pouch."

"That's good." Grandfather Knox placed his hand on Aaron's shoulder with an approving smile.

Aaron was anxious to hear about the power of the coyote. "I'm not sure what it all means. Can you help me with that, Grandfather?"

Grandfather Knox nodded his head in acknowledgment. "I can tell you what the coyote symbolizes. It is up to you to choose in what direction you would like to go as you travel through life."

"The Coyote is clever, intelligent, and persistent. You must decide what you would like to accomplish in your lifetime, what is most important to you. The coyote symbolizes skill as well as persistence in reaching goals to ensure that the end result is not overshadowed by indecisiveness. As is true of the coyote, your environment will always be influential in your life's satisfaction. Be sure your roots are planted in earth that is one with your spirit. As you move through life, think of the strengths of the quick moving, unpredictable coyote. Slow down and try to connect to your spirit when making decisions. Remember, too, that the coyote is known as the trickster."

Aaron didn't completely understand and wanted to know more. "Grandfather, what do you mean by trickster?"

Grandfather placed his chin in his hand and tapped the table slowly with one finger as he thought. "If your life is going in the wrong direction the coyote will get your attention in unexpected ways. It could be a trick to confuse you and make you think about the choices you are making."

After Aaron's breakfast feast and the information shared by his grandfather, he went to his room to record the details of his Quest. He chronicled the experience in his sacred space; the days of fasting, his intimate connection to nature, and the appearance of his totem animal. Aaron recorded his grandfather's words of wisdom and all that the spirit of the coyote represented. It was a lot to think about in such a short period of time, but he now felt more like a man than a boy and stronger because of the experience. He was sure that one day he would share the details of his Vision Quest with his son.

*    *    *    *    *

High school went by quickly for Aaron. He was a star athlete on the football team. His quickness of movement and natural unpredictability often left the opposing players at a loss.

Choosing his college program was easy. He loved everything about the White Mountains National Forest and wanted to protect and maintain it, just as he had imagined when he was a boy. He was offered the position of forest ranger when he graduated from college, fulfilling his lifelong dream. After five years his experience and natural ability was rewarded, and he was promoted to Forest Supervisor, the job of his dreams.

*    *    *    *    *

Winters in New Hampshire often brought icy driving conditions, but natives of the area knew how to maneuver the ruts, twisting dirt roads, and fallen rocks with ease. Aaron had always been comfortable traveling the roughly cut roadways and trails, even in conditions that changed often, quickly, and dramatically. He had the instincts of the Native American, confirming he was intuitively connected to the land of his ancestors.

After the accident, the investigation determined that the truck he drove up the mountain that day had a mechanical defect that challenged its stability. It was the truck he usually took, number 4433. It was Aaron's custom to do a circle check before driving any National Forest vehicle; walking completely around it, checking the tire pressure, looking for any issues that needed to be taken care of ahead of time. The truck displayed the White Mountain National Forest logo, and it was important to Aaron that everything was in perfect condition. Anna knew his routine and was sure that he would have completed the check, just as he always did, before he left for the mountain.

The early report indicated that the truck's driveshaft was unstable and the trip up the mountain escalated the mechanical deterioration. It was determined that as Aaron drove up the mountainside that morning control of the truck became impossible. The terrain was challenging even in the best of weather conditions. Weather reports documented darkening skies and confirmed snow warnings for the approximate time he was on the narrow, mountain road. Anna could only imagine that he decided to drive to the top and seek shelter rather than pulling over, but he never made it.

The day of the accident began like any other day. That afternoon Anna sat in the kitchen of their farm style home, with the front door open, watching for Aaron's return after a long workday. A glass of red wine was waiting, and supper was almost ready. She was making chicken parmesan, his favorite. From the front window, she could see the familiar National Forest truck as it turned down the dirt road, kicking up a cloud of dust. Anna was sure it was Aaron. She couldn't help but smile as Bud, Max and Cayenne happily ran to welcome him, but was surprised when Aaron didn't get out of the truck. Two of their ranger friends, Bill and Ted, jumped out and waived to her. Anna walked to the door and stepped onto the snow covered front porch. The strong, late afternoon breeze stung her face as dark, heavy, storm clouds moved slowly across the sky. It looked to her like another storm was on its way.

"Aaron isn't home yet, but why don't you join us for dinner? There's plenty," Anna said with a smile. "Oh, yes, and there's wine!"

But she could see her friends' eyes were intense, and their faces were tense and serious.

"What's wrong?" she asked quickly.

Anna began to feel anxious and was only vaguely aware that Bud, Max, and Cayenne were making high-pitched crying noises as they circled around her.

Ted held out his arm, directing her to the truck. "There's been an accident. You need to come with us right now."

They didn't have to say more. Anna sensed it was urgent. It had to be Aaron. Quickly, she stepped back into the house, turned off the stove, grabbed her bag, rounded the boys up and locked the door. Ted left the front passenger seat of the truck for her, and he slipped into the back seat. Bill drove.

Anna took a deep breath. "How bad is it?"

Bill spoke calmly and carefully. "He was almost to the top of Great Gulf and something happened. We know the wind velocity changed and a sudden snow squall came through. There must have been a mechanical failure in the truck. Aaron was too good not to be able to jockey the road. It looks like the truck could not make the curve and plummeted to the ridge below."

Bill's voice cracked as he described what they believed happened. The truth was, at this point, they really didn't have all the facts. It was all conjecture. It wasn't until months later that the details of the accident were confirmed. What they did know, what they could tell her for sure that night, was that Aaron was in ICU in a coma fighting for his life.

Snow began to fall, swirling and blowing, as they made their way to the hospital. Anna felt her stomach turn and her muscles tighten. She closed her eyes and listened to Ted and Bill talk about what they thought happened. She wanted to cry, but her fear didn't allow tears; not yet, not now. Anna had to see Aaron. She would know by looking at him how bad he really was.

The drive to the hospital seemed endless. When they arrived at Memorial Hospital in North Conway, they were told that Aaron had taken a turn for the worse and was medevacked to the Dartmouth Hitchcock trauma center. Again, Anna's stomach tightened, this time bringing waves of nausea.

She closed her eyes and prayed. "Let him live, please. Just let him live."

It was a two-hour drive from the hospital to the trauma center, but Bill wasn't interested in the speed limit and got them there in record time in spite of the accumulating snow.

Anna tried to control her nausea and the panicked, screaming voice in her head. When they entered the hospital room she stopped to collect herself before moving toward the bed. The room was stark with hard, fluorescent, overhead lighting. Standing over the unrecognizable figure she prayed someone had made a mistake, but his wedding band was a match to Aaron's.

Anna's vision was blurred by her tears. Could it be the unthinkable was real and it was her husband lying in the bed before her? Was it Aaron? His head was wrapped in bandages and his face was battered and bruised beyond recognition.

Somewhere in the room she heard a doctor's voice describing his injuries. She tried to focus on what he was saying, but the man she loved was lying in front of her, hooked up to a machine that was assisting his breathing. His head was fractured in several places. She heard the doctor say they removed a piece of his scull to reduce the pressure on his brain. It was surgically secured in his stomach until it was safe to replace it. A second cranial surgery would then be necessary. They didn't know the extent of the brain injury, and that could not be determined until - or if he came out of the coma.

When she touched his hand, his skin felt cool and stiff. His facial trauma left grotesque, black and purple swelling and bruising that took her breath away. His eyes were sunken deeply beneath lids engorged with blood. One cheekbone had been crushed and the surgery necessary to repair it could not be performed until his condition improved. Both arms and legs had multiple breaks and were in casts and tubes and monitors surrounded his bed. He had been given the last rights but, he was still alive. Anna sat by his bed listening to the beep, beep, beep of the monitor, staring at the unrecognizable man lying in the bed.

Her mind raced. Maybe they had made a mistake. Maybe it wasn't Aaron. It could be a man who had the same wedding band. Aaron might be home now wondering where she was. That made sense, he was at home.

Anna left the ICU and dumped her bag upside down on the table in the waiting room looking for her cell phone. She had to call him and let him know where she was. She had to tell him about the terrible mistake.

Her voice quivered. "Where is my phone? I know it's here somewhere."

Anna was sure Aaron was worried about her. She was always home when he arrived for dinner. Finding her phone, she dialed quickly. In her hast she missed numbers and got an error message. Again, she dialed. Taking her time, she dialed slowly, carefully making sure to get the numbers right. The phone rang, again, and again, and again. The voice message – Aaron's voice, interrupted the ringing. He did not answer.

A tall man in a suit and tie entered the room. "I'm Doctor Welsh. We have to talk."

Anna was not ready to hear anything he had to say. She stepped back. The wall at the entrance to the ICU stopped her movement abruptly. It felt cold and hard.

She heard herself say, "Tomorrow, he'll be better tomorrow."

The doctor, speaking softly and shaking his head in agreement said, "The next twenty-four hours are critical. We'll talk tomorrow."

Anna returned to Aaron's bedside, stiffly settling into the chair close by the head of his bed.

She prayed. "Please, Aaron, just keep breathing."

The beep, beep, beep of the monitors lulled her into a deep, fitful sleep. Sitting in the chair she slept and woke throughout the night. Nurses came and went checking Aaron's vital signs and watching for change. They were kind to Anna, asking if she needed a drink or something to eat, but food was the furthest thing from her mind.

Ted and Bill sat outside in the visitors' room sleeping from time to time, drinking coffee, and checking to see if Anna needed anything. She wanted to smile at them and thank them for all they had done, but she couldn't smile. She could only stare at Aaron's lifeless body lying in the bed.

As day broke, Ted and Bill got ready to leave. They said they would take care of the boys and be back that evening. Anna choked down the black coffee and ate half of the donut they brought to her before they left. She couldn't taste anything, nor could she feel anything. The beep, beep, beep of the monitor was her constant companion.

"Please, just let him live," she prayed over and over again.

As promised, Doctor Welsh returned for their talk.

She heard the words, "He is not responding. He cannot breathe on his own. It will take time for the brain swelling to go down. We'll know more then. I don't want to give you false hope but, in cases like these, it could go either way. Be prepared."

Anna moved her head slowly to indicate she understood. The reality was they didn't know anything. The beep, beep, beep of the monitors echoed in her brain. Her body softened, she closed her eyes, and finally cried. She cried until she could not breathe. Anna was inconsolable. A nurse who had been watching her closely entered the room and gave her a glass of water and a box of tissues, wrapping her arm around her. Anna could hear herself sobbing but had no control over her tears. She felt strangely like a bystander watching a bizarre play. Her sadness came in waves, moving through her body as she cried to exhaustion. The nurse consoled her while holding her gently. Anna rested her head on the nurse's shoulder, crying until she could cry no more.

Anna didn't know the nurse. She wanted to ask her name, but she couldn't speak. Her eyes, red and swollen, searched the nurse's face. It was kind and wise. She could see the nurse was crying with her, sharing her pain.

\*     \*     \*     \*     \*

Days turned into weeks. Anna spent most of her time by Aaron's bed waiting for something to change. He had several seizures, and his brain function remained minimal. The doctor suggested she think about taking him off life support. They had no reason to believe he would improve. The doctor warned that there was a strong possibility of infection, more seizures, and pneumonia. He felt it was unrealistic to expect his brain function to return.

Anna was thankful he was still breathing, even if it wasn't on his own. She read to him, talked about what was happening in the world, and said, "I love you" at least one hundred times a day. Nothing changed.

Bill and Ted visited regularly at first. They were taking care of the boys for Anna, but their visits were further and further apart and brief. Anna understood. She began going to the hospital later and leaving earlier. When Aaron's condition was stable, he was moved back to Memorial Hospital, which was closer to home and made Anna's visits more convenient.

\*　　\*　　\*　　\*　　\*

At home Anna walked from room to room forgetting what she was looking for. Bud, Max, and Cayenne followed her every move. She forgot to water the plants, and they died. The holidays were approaching, but they were not important to her this year. She had no tree, no lights. Her nights were mostly sleepless as she tossed and turned. When her body finally surrendered to sleep, she often awoke not quite sure what time or day it was.

After two months with no change in Aaron's condition, Anna returned to work. She had been submerged in the antiseptic hospital environment and the incessant beep, beep, beep of the hospital equipment. It was time for some kind of normalcy in her life.

Returning to work at the newspaper forced Anna to get out of bed and organize her day around something other than watching Aaron breathe. The last two months left her chronically tired, unable eat, and she had lost weight. Terri, noticing the dramatic change in her appearance, called her into the office and asked her to sit down.

Looking directly at Anna, she spoke in a stern, authoritarian voice. "You need to see your doctor. Make an appointment today. I will take you. That's an order."

Anna knew she was right and agreed.

The following week the doctor examined her and ran a battery of tests. She sat in the little examination room in a paper Johnny waiting for the results. Anna knew it was stress; stress was making her sick, causing the exhaustion, the nausea, the constant, uncontrollable crying. She was certain as soon as Aaron woke up it would stop.

The doctor knocked on the door and entered, putting her at ease with a warm smile.

She was not prepared for what came next. "Congratulations, Anna, you are going to be a mother."

Anna heard the words, but had trouble understanding them. "Did you say I'm going to be a mother? Are you saying I'm pregnant?"

She felt a wave in the pit of her stomach rise up as she said the words out loud. "I'm going to have a baby?"

The doctor took her hand. "Yes, Anna, you are going to have a baby. You are slightly anemic, so I want you to take prenatal vitamins. I know you have been through a lot and are still struggle with your husband's condition, but you have to think about your baby now. Your husband would want you to."

Anna repeated the words. "Aaron and I are going to have a baby."

For the first time in a very long time she felt light and hopeful. She felt like her whole body was smiling. He had to wake up now, didn't he? They were going to have a baby.

The doctor's secretary gave her a date and time for her next appointment, including a sonogram. At that time, she would find out if they were going to have a son or a daughter. Anna was sure he would have to come back to her now.

Anna and Terri went to lunch after her doctor's appointment.

Terri had been concerned about Anna's health since the accident. "Alright, Anna, what's going on? Is everything okay?"

Anna's face lit up. "Aaron and I are going to have a baby. I'm due in June."

Anna began to laugh. At first a quite giggle, but it soon turned into an uncontrollable belly laugh. Terri joined in as they hugged, laughed, and cried tears of joy.

Anna tried to choke down a glass of milk and a sandwich. She covered her mouth as she gagged slightly. "I'd better get this prescription filled. My stomach is not being nice to me right now."

Terri suggested that she try a protein drink. "My friend, Beth, had morning sickness for the first three months of her pregnancy, and the drinks seemed to make a difference."

Anna agreed to give it a try. This was new territory; she had given up on the thought of children many years ago. Now, suddenly, she was going to be a mother. She said goodbye to Terri, promising to be in work first thing in the morning with a protein drink, or two, and then she headed to the hospital. It was time to have a different kind of talk with Aaron.

*     *     *     *     *

The hospital room was the same one he had been in for many weeks. Cards from friends were on the wall, others were placed in a line on the bureau, so that the name of the sender could be seen from his bed. Flowers and plants lined the windowsill. A brightly colored quilt, made by his mother, lay across the foot of his bed. Aaron's body was still. His chest moved slowly up and down with each machine-driven breath he took. But today - today felt different to Anna. Today she didn't come alone; she came with their baby inside her. Anna sat in her chair, the one she always sat in, the one by the head of his bed.

She reached out and gently pushed Aaron's hair from his forehead. The swelling and bruising were gone, and his handsome face looked peaceful.

She spoke softly. "We are going to have a baby, my love. You need to return to us. He or she needs you as much as I do. Please come back to us - your family, please."

The beep, beep, beep of the monitor echoed through the silence.

Anna smiled. "We have so much to do before our baby is born. I need your help. In a few weeks, we'll know if it's a boy or a girl. Do you want a son or a daughter? Of course, I know what you'd say, 'As long as our baby is healthy, that's all that matters.' We'll need a name, too. We'll have to think about that."

She leaned forward and slipped her hand into his. It was cool to the touch, soft, lifeless. The beep, beep, beep melted into the background.

Anna moved her chair closer. "That back room, right near our bedroom, will work perfectly. All it needs is a coat of paint, pretty curtains, a small bureau, and a rocker. I've always thought that when the time came I'd like a swing set in the back yard, right by the Lilac bush. That would be perfect. That's it. I always imagined a swing set right there. I like the one that has the fort attached. I know I'm getting ahead of myself, but I'm so happy. Please come back to us and be happy, too."

She kissed his cheek and turned to leave, passing nurses in the hallway that she now knew on a first name basis.

*    *    *    *    *

At home, Anna was greeted at the door by the boys; Bud, Max and Cayenne. She noticed that even the house felt different now, lighter, cheerier. The boys followed her up the stairs to the bedroom where she slipped into jeans and a tee-shirt. Looking at herself in the mirror she pulled her shirt up to peek at her still flat belly, imagining her baby inside. Barefoot, she walked down the little hall to the back room, the baby's room. It was the perfect size. She envisioned a bureau, crib, bookcase, a rocker in the corner, and toys - lots of toys.

Anna straightened with a start. She thought she heard Aaron's voice.

Turning, she searched the room. "Wow, I could have sworn."

Again, she heard his voice.

He was saying, "Sky."

Anna heard it again, "Sky".

Sky was Aaron's mother's name. He always spoke of his mother lovingly. She and his stepfather sold the farm years before and moved to Arizona, retiring from farm life. He missed her, but he knew her life was full and she was happy.

Sky immediately flew back to New Hampshire to be with Anna and Aaron after the accident. After several weeks passed with no change, she reluctantly returned home. Anna promised she would be the first to know when Aaron opened his eyes.

Anna understood what he was telling her. "We are going to have a baby girl, and Sky will be her name."

*    *    *    *    *

The day of the sonogram came quickly. Anna worked until an hour before her appointment, choked down a protein drink, and headed to the doctor's office. Her belly wasn't very big yet, but she loved the little, growing bump. The nurse assured Anna that the sonogram would not hurt the baby. She laid back, exposed her belly, and watched as the nurse applied a cool, jelly-like substance. Placing the wand on her stomach, the nurse slowly moved it back and forth. A large computer screen next to the bed was facing Anna so she, too, could see the image. The picture was a bit grainy, but once the nurse pointed out the form, Anna could see what looked like the baby's head, body, and tiny hands and feet. Looking closely, she noticed a movement that looked like a kick.

"Hi, Sky," she said out loud.

The nurse nodded. "It looks like you're going to have a girl."

"I know. He told me."

"Who told you?" asked the nurse.

"My husband, he told me right after my first doctor's appointment."

The nurse smiled, accepting Anna's information without question.

It was fun for Anna to think about the baby and everything she and Aaron were going to do when she was born. They would have a big christening, inviting all their friends. Ted and Bill would be there. They had supported her every step of the way since the accident. Her editor and friend, Terri, give her time off from work whenever she needed it for hospital and doctor's visits. Every time Aaron ran a fever or seized, Bill came to her side and assure her she was not alone and everything would be okay. Anna still refused to accept that Aaron would never come out of the coma, even though the doctors told her otherwise. She felt he had to - to meet Sky.

*     *     *     *     *

Anna put the sonogram on her refrigerator where she could look at it regularly. Over the next several weeks as her belly grew she began to show and, at last, the morning sickness passed. Finally, she was able to eat everything and anything she wanted without getting sick. Her weight was perfect. She was feeling good, and her pregnancy was going according to schedule.

Anna had fun as she prepared the baby's room. Bill helped her put the crib together: a white, spindled masterpiece with a slightly curved side rail and a head and footboard that made it look a little like a sleigh. Overhead, white netting flowed from a wire hoop, forming a canopy that softly framed where the little princess would sleep. Bill carefully moved the furniture she bought into the little room down the hall, and they arranged each piece with expert precision.

Terri stopped in with food and to lend a hand. When everything was in place they could see that Anna was pleased. Mission accomplished. By the end of the evening they admired their work and toasted to the completion of the baby's room. Anna's toast was a wine glass filled with lemon water.

When it was time to leave, Anna walked Bill and Terri to the door, thanked them, and watched as the boys accompanied them to their cars. Once there, they quickly returned to Anna's side as she waved goodbye, watching until their cars disappeared into the sunset. It was fun for Anna to think about her new baby daughter. The white, baby furniture reflect light and, to her, represented hope for the future - their future.

Evenings were still lonely. Sometimes Anna fell into a deep sleep waking only when the morning light peeked into her bedroom window. Some nights she dreamed of Aaron with his arms wrapped around her. Those were the nights she slept best and were the dreams she didn't want to wake up from.

When unable to sleep, she looked through her photo albums, photos of Aaron and her when they were dating. They looked so young. A high school football game and a spilled drink brought them together. Anna and her girlfriend, Margo, were in the stands during a big, home game. Anna attempted to pass a cola to Margo who was sitting at the end of the bench. She stretched just a little bit further than her balance allowed. The soda-filled paper cup dropped out of her hand and landed right in Aaron's lap, soaking him. Anna stepped back horrified when she realized what had happened, but in seconds was choking back a laugh.

He looked up at her, eyes twinkling, dimple flashing and said, "Now, that feels wet!"

Embarrassed, she tipped her head and glanced up at him with a flirty grin. They shared a laugh as she apologized for her clumsiness. Aaron placed his ball cap on his lap and shrugged his shoulders. It was like at first sight for them both. They dated off and on for a year, but lost touch when graduation took them in different directions.

Anna's plan was to be an English teacher. Aaron's goal was a career in forestry, his first love. He was focused on working in the White Mountain National Forest.

Anna and Aaron ran into each other again after college, at the same football field where they first met. Both had just ended unsatisfying relationships and were still a little guarded about getting involved in another one.

The Thanksgiving Day game was big in the community, and they were both there with friends to cheer their home team on. Nothing was spilled this time, but they knew at once they would not lose track of each other again. It didn't take long for their love to bloom, only six months later Aaron asked Anna to marry him. She was not surprised, and the ring was exactly what she wanted.

*    *    *    *    *

Right from the start there was no question that they were going to live in New Hampshire. Anna, originally from California, was comfortable with big city life and all its busyness and noise. But, she chose and was accepted into the teaching program at Plymouth State University in New Hampshire, and fell in love with the White Mountains.

On her first visit, she felt like she had come home. Anna worked at a local pub during the summer and discovered that she enjoyed the cooler, beautifully colored seasons of the Northeast. When she took her first ski lesson she was hooked, and it wasn't long before snowboarding became her second all-time favorite sport. By the time she graduated she had impressive skills and New Hampshire was her new home.

*     *     *     *     *

Once the wedding date was chosen, they set their hearts on finding the perfect place to live. After long, heartfelt discussions about their future family, they agreed a home with enough bedrooms for their three children fit their vision. It also needed to be warm and welcoming to all who visited. After looking at several properties that didn't feel right to them, they entertained the idea of renting for a while.

By chance, Aaron drove past a house with a for sale sign posted on the entry to a driveway. He noticed the friendly, warp around porch and what looked like a cement sculpture of a coyote guarding the front door. He decided to take a look. The dirt driveway led him to a white farmhouse with bright red shutters and a large red barn. It reminded him of the Knox family homestead where he grew up, and he wanted to take a look inside right away.

When the real estate agent brought them through the five-room farm house it captured their hearts. It was perfect for them; there was an updated country kitchen with stainless steel appliances, and a breakfast bar, all beautifully accented by a large picture window over the sink looking out into the back yard. A winding road leading to the dirt driveway introduced the home site, and the magnificent mountain backdrop completed the captivating location.

Aaron especially liked the large dining room's sliding doors that opened onto a cobblestone patio. He imagined himself cooking for the family outside on the grill. The first-floor bathroom was a plus, too. Upstairs there was a large master bedroom, a smaller second bedroom, and another full bathroom. The house was built in the early nineteen-hundreds, immediately apparent by the large boulders that formed the foundation and reflected the rock walls scattered throughout the property. There was also a big red barn, chicken coop, and a fenced in area that at one time must have been a lively barnyard. Although the homestead was tucked into the woods on four acres of land, it was easily accessible from the main road. There was room for a large garden and whatever else they wanted to add. Behind the barn was a spring fed pond, complete with viewing bench. They knew immediately this was their home. Here is where they wanted to raise their family. They could easily add on as their needs and family grew.

The wedding plans were simple, only close friends and family. Aaron's mom and stepdad flew in from their retirement community in Arizona. Margo, who was with Anna when she first met Aaron, was her maid of honor. Lung cancer claimed

Anna's dad's life when she was a senior in high school, but her mom flew in from California to give her away. The celebration was bittersweet for her mother, but Aaron immediately stole her heart. They were all family right from the start.

Bill, the best man, was there with his new wife of only a few months. Aaron and he went to forestry school together at Plymouth State University in New Hampshire, and both were now employed by the U.S. Forest Station in the White Mountains. They looked somewhat alike with the same large frame and dark coloring, often taken as brothers. Bill was very excited for his brother from another mother, and was happy to stand up for him, just as Aaron had done for Bill only a few months earlier.

The mild October morning was perfect for their wedding. They married on a mountaintop surrounded by a rainbow of fall colors and a sky that sparkled with sunshine. It was a simple ceremony followed by great food, lively music, and a joy filled celebration at their new home. The exceptional weather allowed the party to flow onto the patio, continuing into the early hours of the morning.

A honeymoon in Aruba was just what they needed after the rush of wedding plans, the move to their new home, and their perfect ceremony. They ate, drank, played in the sun, and made love, celebrating their new life together.

The return flight touched down at Logan Airport in Boston. It was a clear, cool fall evening. On the three-hour drive home, they talked about what their life was going to be like. Aaron had the perfect job and their home was everything they wanted. Anna, however, was still job searching and was not sure in what direction she was going to go.

As they turn down the winding road that led home, the change in season was evident. The brightly colored leaves that decorated the trees when they left for their honeymoon had fallen, forming a burnt orange carpet that lead to their front steps. The outside light was on, brightening up their front walkway. A bottle of champagne sat outside on the porch by the front door, silently guarded by the cement coyote.

The note attached read, "Welcome home. You two are very special and deserve all that is good in life. Enjoy!! Bill."

Aaron unlocked the door and scooped Anna up into his arms, carrying her over the threshold and into the house.

The next morning, they extended their honeymoon by sleeping late, making love, and sipping mimosas while eating breakfast in their robes. Life was good, and they were gratefully enjoying every minute of it.

\*     \*     \*     \*     \*

Anna flipped through the newspaper. "I don't know what I'm going to do, Aaron. I thought I would be working by now."

The conversation was interrupted by the buzz of her cell phone.

It was Bill. "Hi Anna, I know you guys just got back from your honeymoon, but I wanted to say welcome home. I'm sure you two enjoyed yourselves. I have something you might be interested in. You know my sister, Terri. She's the editor of the local newspaper, The Reporter. Yesterday afternoon she mentioned that they were looking for a reporter. I know you don't have a job yet, so I mentioned your name. It might be a good fit. If you're interested, why don't you give her a call. Do it as quickly as possible, there are others who want the position."

Anna was surprised. "Thank you for thinking of me, Bill. Let me think about it. I promise I'll call her."

Bill again emphasized how important it was for her to call Terri back as soon as possible. "Tell Aaron I'll see him on Wednesday at the station."

Anna thanked him for putting on the light for them and for the bottle of champagne. "That was such a nice surprise. It was the perfect welcome home."

Anna wanted to talk to Aaron about the job with the newspaper. She wasn't sure if she could do it, or even wanted to.

Aaron surprised her. "I think you should talk to Terri about the reporter job, and see how you feel. What's the worst thing that can happen? You can tell her you're not interested if that's how you feel. But, maybe it will work for you, even if it's for just a little while."

That afternoon Anna spoke to Terri about the job and found out it was full-time. Anna's background was a good fit and, after a brief conversation, Terri offered her the position. It wasn't what Anna expected to be doing when she graduated from college, but she thought working as a newspaper reporter might be interesting. She was surprised and excited about the unexpected challenge. Anna had applied to the local school system, but there were no full-time openings as she had hoped. After some discussion, she and Aaron decided that the job at the newspaper was the right move for her, meanwhile, she could go back to school for her Master's.

"Yes," Anna agreed with Aaron, "that will work."

*     *     *     *     *

It all seemed so long ago. She thought it surreal that she was revisiting their life by way of their photo albums. There were pictures of vacations they took together over the years; Aaron wearing goofy hats and looking quite dashing in outrageous poses. Anna's petite frame, light complexion, and blonde hair, was a sharp contrasted to his six-foot, two-inch, dark hair, and large physique. He was funny and outgoing. Anna was quiet and introspective with a dry sense of humor. They worked and played well together. Anna watched their life unfold in the photos, enjoying and reliving them as she flipped through each page.

Anna couldn't help but laugh at pictures capturing the arrival of Bud, Max and Cayenne. The photos chronicled their life and growth from sweet, little puppies to the beautiful boys they were today.

Even the delivery of their chickens was captured in photos. Aaron and Anna populated the coop as the boys tried to figure out what they were supposed to do with the little creatures that were running around the barnyard. The memories made her feel better, closer to Aaron. Their life had been good, filled with love, friends, and adventures.

Photos of Bill, Ted, and Terri filled many of the pages, recording the celebrations and events they all shared over the years of friendship. Ted married his high school sweetheart and was now the father of three boys. His wife, Gail, a teacher, worked in the local elementary school. Ted had a bit of a roving eye but, from what Anna could tell, he was harmless.

Terri, now Anna's boss and good friend, was married for a while but, as she often said, "It just didn't take."

Terri also had an attraction to women. Currently, her partner, Nancy, lived in Southern New Hampshire. They got together a couple of weekends a month and that seemed to be working for them.

Bill married his high school sweetheart, but life was not kind. After only two years of marriage Bill lost his wife to cancer. He never seemed to recover from the loss. Bill dated occasionally over the years, but never for long. He was the man everyone called on for help, showing up, helping out, and never looked for anything in return. Anna hoped he would find someone to love. He always seemed sad to her.

Anna was sure if she had it to do over again she would not change one thing about Aaron and their life together, and she knew their friends missed him almost as much as she did.

The boys lay across the bed waiting for her to turn off the light and call it a night. Some nights were longer than others, but tonight she could feel the baby kicking and that made her happy.

"Hi, Sky," she said, stroking her belly. "I can't wait to meet you. I'm sure your daddy wants to meet you, too."

Sleep finally came, offering her peace after a long day.

*    *    *    *    *

Morning arrived, and it was time to greet the day. Anna stretched, as the boys moved off the bed and rushed down the stairs to the back door waiting to go out. When downstairs she unlatched the door, and they scooted by her, anxious for their morning romp. This morning Anna had two assignments for the newspaper; one was to cover a new business opening on Main Street, and the other was to visit one of her favorite hometown celebrations.

Old Home Days were a New Hampshire tradition that flowered in the late 1800s through a public-relations campaign initiated by the then Governor Rollins. Its aim was to support small-town life. The celebration kicking off today was for Plymouth where her newspaper's offices were located. It would be a full day.

Anna peeked out the window. The sky was dark and the leaves on the trees were swaying frantically in the morning's erratic gusts of wind. It had been hot and muggy for several days. A ping on her cell phone flashed and announced, "thunderstorms and flood warnings."

"That's not going to be good for today's Old Home Day," she said thinking out loud.

Before Anna headed for Plymouth to cover the first event, she opened the back door to let the boys in. They quickly pushed by her and headed towards their bowls. A clap of thunder broke the silence, and she reminded herself to close the windows before she left.

"I need to check the upstairs windows, too." she said, speaking offhand to the boys.

From the patio doors off the dining room Anna could see across the yard to the barn. It had become Aaron's man cave of sorts. He spent his spare time there, handcrafting pieces of wood, creating walking sticks and wooden figures intended for local craft fairs. She lingered, imagining the barn doors opened wide just as they were when he was inside working on one of his creations.

Looking up she could see the sky was black and grey and angry clouds made their presence known as far as the eye could see. Anna grabbed her umbrella hurrying out the door. The boys would stay in until she returned home later that afternoon. A flash of lighting flew across the sky followed by a loud clap of thunder, but still no rain.

When she arrived at the Old Home Day site it hadn't rained there either, but the thunder continued to echo and flashes of lighting scattered across the sky. Finding her contact person, Anna asked some questions and took notes. The field was decorated with kiosks and tents that housed the arts and crafts of local artisans, including homemade pastries and canned goods of all varieties. Beginning in July, individual communities in the area scheduled a weekend to offer the fun, carnival-like event. Anna covered every one of them for the past several years. There was always something different, something unique about each of them, but this weather was not good for a successful turnout.

The sky quieted as Anna took pictures and visited the vendors. Old Home Days were always fun to write about. She could see the attendance was small, but it was still early, and storm warnings were probably keeping people away. She knew if the weather cleared it would be busy the following day. Anna was there for over an hour talking to visitors, vendors, and taking pictures for the newspaper spread. The story would be on the front page above the fold, as it always was.

Her next stop was a scheduled interview with the owners of a new business on Main Street. They were happy that the newspaper was covering their grand opening; talking candidly about the challenges of a startup business and expressing excitement about moving in the direction of their dreams. The new business was evidence to Anna that the economy was picking up.

*　　*　　*　　*　　*

Anna's mood was light and hopeful when she stopped at the hospital to see Aaron. The nurses had just given him a bath and dressed him. His face was soft and expressionless. She no longer noticed the beep, beep of the monitors. Anna sat in her chair and stroked his head taking a long, deep breath, wondering how many times had she done it before expecting him to respond.

She spoke softly. "Hi, honey, we're here. It looks like there's a storm brewing. Do you remember the kayak trip we took down the river? The river was shallow, and we had to pull the kayaks across the sand bar. It wasn't long before the rains came. We were soaked from head to toe from river water mixed with pouring rain. As quickly as the rain came it stopped, the sun came out, and it was warm and beautiful again. It was a wonderful storm. I would share a storm with you again any time. Please come back to us. We need you."

Tears rolled down her cheeks. She hadn't cried in a long time. The baby kicked. Standing, Anna lifted Aaron's hand and put it on her belly. There was another kick, but no response from Aaron - nothing. Returning his arm gently to his side she kissed his forehead and left, feeling deserted and alone.

*    *    *    *    *

Anna's drive home was tear-filled. She knew she was feeling sorry for herself, but tried to remember that she had a lot to be thankful for. After all, Sky would soon be born.

Home again, she let the boys out and thought about dinner. Terri called with questions about the two articles she was writing that day, and asked if she would cover two more before the end of the week.

Anna wanted to keep busy. "Yes, that's fine. I feel good."

She made a note to herself as she listened to Terri's talking points.

Anna didn't feel like being alone. "Terri, how about joining me for dinner?"

Terri was hesitant. "Not tonight, I have to talk to Nancy. I think this relationship is winding down, but it's okay. I just realized that I need more time from her than she is willing to give me. I'm feeling sad, but I'll be relieved after we have the talk. I know it's time. Why don't we make a plan for tomorrow night?"

It was just going to be Anna and the boys. She decided it was for the best. Her ankles were a little swollen, and she was tired. A cup of soup and a sandwich was all she had the desire for. The boys came in from their run and another storm warning flashed on her phone as the sky once again darkened. She awkwardly bent over and filled their dishes. After working to stand again, she placed her hand on her aching back and gave it a rub.

Anna confided in her oldest boy, Bud. "I think I'd better get some candles and find a flashlight, just in case we lose our electricity."

He tipped his head to one side trying to understand her every word, snorting in response.

Limping slightly, she walked from the kitchen down the hallway to the back of the house. "I think I have everything I need in the back room."

The mud room was the first addition they made to the farmhouse, adding it soon after they moved in. The new space held the washer and dryer, a wet sink, and cabinets for storage. There was a door that opened to the back yard introducing the cobblestone path that led to the flower garden. Glancing out of the window for just a moment she saw a small coyote sitting in the garden, facing the back door.

Looking at Cayenne, the most aggressive of the boys, she pointed her finger toward the coyote who was still sitting motionless. "I'm glad you're in the house. You would be chasing that little guy out of the garden for sure."

Beside the dryer she found her little stool and used it to reach the top shelf. Climbing up, she opened the cabinet door and found everything she was looking for.

At that moment Anna was startled by a familiar voice. "Get out of there now!"

She looked around. The boys were standing in the doorway waiting for her to return to the kitchen.

Again, she heard, "Get out of there now!"

Grabbing the flashlight and several candles Anna quickly moved to the kitchen. Bud, Max, and Cayenne anxiously followed. She moved to the sink and, leaning against it, peered out the window. Suddenly there was an unsettling rumble and a crashing boom of thunder that echoed and reverberated the floor beneath her feet. Anna knew immediately the house had been struck by lightning.

As she watched smoke billowing from the back of the house, she dialed 9-1-1. Anna herded the boys out through the front door. Her body quivered as she stood in the front yard surrounded by her guardians whose ears were pinned back on alert. Sirens cried out announcing the arrival of the pump trucks. The rural location meant water had to be brought to the site to quell the fire. The trucks arrived quickly and immediately went to work limiting the damage and ending the threat to the rest of the house. When they were done the fire had been squelched and the mud room was boarded off.

Hearing the broadcast over the forest station's radio, Bill arrived on the scene soon after the pump truck.

Speaking with gentle authority Bill said, "I'll take you to Terri's for tonight. The fire could ignite again, and the smell of smoke is heavy and needs to dissipate. They'll be bringing industrial fans to get rid of the smoke. Your mud room can be rebuilt. Don't worry, it's over now. It's boards and appliances, and all of that can be replaced. The important thing is that you and the boys were not hurt and are safe."

"Yes," Anna agreed. "Aaron warned me, he told me to get out of there."

Bill looked at her with a furrowed brow.

She could see the disbelief on his face. "Really, I was in the mud room, Bill, and Aaron's voice was loud and clear. He said, 'Get out of there now!'"

Bill tipped his head and squinted his eyes. "I think we need to get you to Terri's for some rest. You've had a tough night."

She and the boys followed Bill to his truck. Anna climbed awkwardly into the front seat and the boys hopped in the back. Looking through the back window as they pulled away, she could see small tufts of smoke rising from the charred boards that once were her mud room. At the end of the driveway she again saw a small, red coyote with large, white triangular ears.

*     *     *     *     *

Anna knew Bill was right, the damage was only to boards, nothing that couldn't be fixed. They were all safe, and she was grateful. When they reached Terri's house tea was ready. The boys settled in, and Anna told Terri it was Aaron who warned her, telling her to get out of the mud room.

Terri touched her hand. "It's good something told you to get out of there. Your instincts are right on."

Anna was too tired to disagree, but she knew in her heart Aaron saved them. It didn't matter what anyone else thought.

The guest room was warm and comfortable. The boys took their usual places on the bed. Exhausted, Anna fell into a deep, restful sleep.

The next day Aaron's words kept echoing in her head. It was him, she knew it. He was communicating with her from his coma. He told her they were going to have a girl, and he was right. He told her what to name their daughter. It didn't matter what Bill or Terri thought, she knew it was Aaron who saved them. He had warned her. She didn't want to think about what would have happened if she and the boys were in mud room when the lightning struck, exploding into fire. It was Aaron who saved them, and she was sure of it.

*     *     *     *     *

Over the months that followed the debris from the fire was cleared away and the mud room rebuilt. Anna was happy with the small changes she made. Now, going into her ninth month, she was doing very little at the newspaper. Occasionally, Terri asked her to do a phone interview, keeping her involved, but not over-whelmed. Today she was going to stop by the office before she and Terri went to lunch. Anna always enjoyed Terri's company and was looking forward to saying hello to her friends at the office. After their lunch, she planned to go to the hospital to visit Aaron. Yesterday was not a good day for him, he had another seizure. The doctor was still advising Anna not to expect anything to change. It had been six months with no improvement, nothing to celebrate.

The newspaper office was located off the main route, down a winding side street. The brick building, with big white pillars on each side of the front stairs, was unusual for the area, but somehow seemed appropriate for a publishing com-pany. After finding a parking space Anna climbed the stairs, stopping to catch her breath before she went in.

As she entered the office, voices rang out, "Surprise!"

All her friends came to celebrate the upcoming birth with gifts, great food, and amusing labor and delivery stories. Her plan was to go shopping the following week for what she needed when she brought Sky home from the hospital. Now, there was nothing that she needed. She laughed, cried, ate, and gave hugs of thanks to all of her friends.

After the baby shower, she drove to the hospital. For some reason, she was dreading her visit. Anna was happy thinking about her daughter who would soon be born and her great family of friends. But the thought of her husband's lifeless body was stealing her joy. Taking a deep breath, she entered his room. As time passed, get well cards stopped coming, and she had taken most of the plants and flowers home. As she entered the room, the familiar beep, beep, beep of the mon-itor echoed in her ears.

Standing beside the bed she began. "Aaron, they gave me a baby shower today - the gals at work. We have everything a newborn could need. It was wonderful."

Most days Anna read to her husband, but not today. The nurse entered the room to give him a shave. Anna shaved Aaron from time to time and was getting better at it. The nurse handed her everything she needed and left the room. Looking closely at his face Anna wondered why - why wouldn't he come back to her – to them?

Questions danced in her head. "If you can tell me we are going to have a baby girl, if you can tell me to get out of the mud room, why - why can't you talk to me now?"

Anna gently patted the warm, moist towel over his face. Slowly, carefully, she applied the shaving cream.

The razor slid easily as she moved his face in tiny increments back and forth, up and down, and then wiped the remaining foam from his face. "There's that handsome face, the face I fell in love with. Where have you gone, Aaron? If I go home to the mud room, will you talk to me again? Help me understand what I have to do to hear your voice again - please."

Anna stepped back with a start as his body arched and the monitors beeped and flashed with urgency. Nurses ran in from every direction as he seized again and again, finally coming to a stop. Anna closed her eyes, turned, and left the room. Standing in the hall she waited to hear the sound of the lonely beep, beep, beep, a welcomed sign that the seizure had finally ended, and he was once again stable. The only question that remained was how much longer she could continue to live waiting for a change that never seemed to happen.

*    *    *    *    *

It was clear to her that Bill and Terri - everyone thought she was imagining things when she said Aaron talked to her. They didn't believe it was Aaron who warned her about the lightning strike or that he told her to name their daughter, Sky, after his mother. They believed she was under a lot of stress, and it was her instincts that got her out of the mud room in time. It was her mother's intuition that told her she was going to have a girl. But, she knew differently, she knew it was Aaron.

Anna was desperate for answers. When she returned home she decided it was time to find out for sure. The messages she was getting were from Aaron, and there was no doubt in her mind. Maybe a psychic could tell her how to help him come back. It would be her secret.

After some searching she found Priscilla on line. The feedback on the website sounded positive, and Anna liked her story. It simply stated that Priscilla had a gift. Since she was a child she had the ability to communicate with those on the other side. The reviews on her website indicated she helped bring peace to loved ones left behind. Anna told herself, if nothing else, she might get a story out of the meeting for the newspaper, but she was hoping for more.

Priscilla did physic readings out of her home. Anna, with the help of her GPS, found it easily. It was a small, modular house, sitting at an angle on a lot with a long circular driveway. An array of pots, which in summer must have held colorful plants and flowers, were covered with snow. The front porch, more like a deck, had copper torches along the railing from end to end. Brown wicker furniture with brightly colored pillows created a seating circle with a small, rod iron table in the middle. To the far end there was a grill, complete with overhead tarp. Anna thought it looked homey and it made her feel more comfortable.

A woman stepped out onto the deck and waved welcome to Anna. She was tall and chubby with a cherub's face. She wore colorfully dramatic makeup and had long, salt and pepper hair. A multi-colored scarf that matched her flowing housedress was wrapped around her head, holding her hair in place at the nape of her neck. Anna smiled, guessing the cartoon-like character to be Priscilla. Now that she actually saw her, she wasn't sure going there was a good idea.

Priscilla invited her into the house and led her to the living room.

Sitting down, Priscilla patted the chair beside her. "Come, sit down beside me, dear."

Anna was a little uncomfortable. "I - I think, maybe - I'm hoping you can help me."

Priscilla again leaned forward and took her hand."Why don't you tell me what it is you think I can help you with."

Anna looked at Priscilla as she searched for the right words. "My husband, Aaron, has been in a coma for six months. The doctors tell me there is little brain activity - but he talks to me. He tells me things. My friends think it's my imagination. Does this sound crazy to you?"

Priscilla leaned forward and spoke softly. "Not even a little bit, dear. I often get messages from people who have passed away many, many years ago. Now, tell me about the first time you heard from him. Let's start there."

Anna described for Priscilla how Aaron told her they were going to have a daughter and what to name her. She felt hurt that everyone thought she was imagining it and knew they were wrong. They were right about her wanting him back, but she was certain it was Aaron's voice she heard, not her imagination. She was positive of it and was hoping Priscilla could help her prove it, even if it was only to herself.

Priscilla listened to each of Anna's contacts from Aaron very carefully. She asked questions about how Anna was feeling each time and wanted specific details about what the dogs were doing when each contact was being made.

"You know, Anna," her voice was strong and steady, "animals are very sensitive and read your emotional state as well as connect with visiting spirits. We need to find out what is really happening here."

They agreed on a date and time for Priscilla to go to the hospital and visit Aaron. Priscilla wasn't making any promises, but she was going to try and communicate with him. There was an awkward hug goodbye before Anna went on her way.

Meeting Priscilla felt right, and she was comfortable with the next step they had planned. The thought that Priscilla might confirm that the voice she heard really was Aaron's and not her imagination, made her happy.

* * * * *

When Anna got home the boys met her at the door. After a quick hello, they scurried outside for their afternoon run. Anna had a car full of baby gifts from her shower but decided to wait for Bill to help her unload them. When evening came she slipped into her pajamas and slippers and went downstairs to the mud room. Moonlight streamed through the large windows. She could see the mountains in all their splendor as the evening's full moon lit up the sky. The house was silent. Anna sat in the chair by the desk now occupying the corner. Her belly was large enough to stop her from moving completely under it, but she could get close enough to rest her arms on top. On the desk was a pile of cards she had taken from Aaron's hospital room, bills, and pictures of Aaron and her with the boys in the back yard. She remembered they were taken by Bill only a year ago on the Fourth of July. They were happy then, filled with life and plans for the future. So much had changed. She didn't recognize her life anymore.

Anna heard the boys at the back door. Reaching out, she pressed the latch, and they came charging past her and ran into the kitchen. Sitting motionless she quietly listened, hoping to hear Aaron's voice, but there was only silence.

Lying in bed she replayed the day's events. Anna thought about her surprise baby shower, her friends, all the beautiful baby gifts, and her visit with Priscilla. When the beep, beep, beep of the monitors crept into her thoughts, she quickly placed her hand on her belly and thought about Sky. Sleep finally came.

*    *    *    *    *

In the morning Anna was feeling a little off. Her back ached, and she didn't want anything to eat. Bill came over early and brought her coffee and a bagel. He then unloaded her car, carefully setting all her gifts in the baby's room. As soon he brought everything in he left to begin his day at the ranger station.

Coffee and a bagel was not what Anna wanted, so she shared a little piece with each of the boys, then went upstairs to organize, fold, and enjoy every baby blanket, onesie, and set of booties she had received at her shower. The little bedroom looked like an ocean of pink.

The backache returned, now stronger and lasting longer. She moved her shoulders from side to side and round and round attempting to stretch her muscles and relieve the pressure she was feeling in her lower back. There was no improvement. In fact, the pain she was feeling turned into pressure that came and went in waves.

She questioned herself, "Can I be in labor? I think it's too soon."

Again, a wave of pressure in her lower back was followed by a short period of relief. "Yes, I'm in labor."

She dialed Terri to tell her the news. "I'll be there in half an hour, and we can time your labor pains together."

By the time Terri arrived the pressure in her back had turned to pain that was taking her breath away, and the waves were only two minutes apart. Anna had already called her doctor, who told her to come to the hospital right away.

He reminded her, "We don't know how long first babies are going to take. It's a little early, and your labor may stop, but let's be safe. Come in as soon as you can."

Terri gently helped Anna into the car while watching her cringe with each labor pain. The hospital was twenty minutes away. In that time, the contractions grew stronger and became closer together. Terri pulled up to the hospital door and called for help. She watched as attendants helped Anna into a wheelchair and pushed her through hospital entryway.

The car parked, Terri settled into the waiting room and watched as Anna was moved to the nearby admissions office. Minutes later she was backed out of admissions and rushed up the hallway through the hospital's large, double doors.

Terri didn't have to wait long for the news. Anna delivered a five pound, eight-ounce, baby girl, only twenty minutes after she arrived at the hospital. Her daughter entered the world a little early and, although small, was perfect in every way.

After making several phone calls Terri headed to Aaron's room, only two floors up from where his wife and new daughter were sleeping. It was her first visit in many months. Terri told the floor nurse the new baby news and asked if she could see Aaron. The nurse gave her the go ahead, adding that there had been no change. Terri walked slowly into the room stopping several feet from his bed.

She wondered why life had dealt him such a difficult hand. "You have a new baby girl, Aaron."

Terri had no desire to move any closer to the bed. As far as she was concerned Aaron had died in the accident. She admired Anna's loyalty but, if it were her, she would have let him go. She turned to leave, almost colliding with Bill who was entering the room.

"I thought I would tell Aaron the news." Bill said awkwardly.

"I just did." Terri was conflicted. "I don't get it. Why does she keep him on life support? He died from that accident, but she refuses to accept it."

Bill shook his head. "I don't know. She keeps saying she hears his voice. I think she wants it so badly she believes it. It's been almost a year and still no change. Anna is hanging on to a dead man."

Terri agreed. "Maybe the baby will make a difference - fill the void."

*    *    *    *    *

The nurse placed Anna's newborn, baby girl in her arms.

The scrunched-up face and mop of dark hair made Anna laugh.

"I don't know who she looks like, but right now she has Aaron's coloring."

She kissed her tiny forehead and, for the first time, breathed in the newborn baby smell.

"Wait until Daddy sees you," she said hugging her daughter close.

The next day, as Anna cradled Sky in her arms, the nurse took her by wheelchair to Aaron's bedside. Anna was still a little weak but wanted to stand so she could move closer to the bed. Bending down slowly, she gently placed their sleeping daughter beside Aaron's motionless body.

Speaking softly, Anna made the introduction. "This is your daughter, Aaron. Sky is beautiful and perfect. She needs her daddy. We need you to come home."

Sky continued to sleep peacefully by Aaron's side. After several minutes Anna slipped her arms under Sky and hugged her tightly as she lifted her from the bed and sat back down in the wheelchair. She hoped Sky would change something for Aaron, but he remained motionless and unresponsive.

Feeling tired, Anna wanted to stop thinking about Aaron just for a while. At that moment, she was happy and grateful for her precious child and their new life. She just wanted to take her home, introduce her to the boys and place Sky in her crib. Anna vowed to keep her safe and tell stories of her father until the day he awoke and returned to them.

*    *    *    *    *

Anna and Sky were healthy and able to leave the hospital in two days. Bill picked them up and drove them home. Terri was waiting to welcome them and help Anna in any way she could. The boys ran to Anna with yelps of joy as she climbed out of the truck.

Bending down to say hello, she stroked each of them and said, "Good boy, I've missed you." They wagged their tails in excitement welcoming her home.

Bill carried the tiny new member of the family carefully into the house and placed the baby seat on the floor, so the boys could take a look. They sniffed and nuzzled her little feet in apparent approval. It was evident that from that moment on Sky had three personal guardians.

It didn't take Anna long before she was feeling strong and able to get back into her pre-pregnancy clothes. She was a little frazzled trying to satisfy her new daughter's eating and sleeping schedule but, over the next few weeks, everything fell into place. Anna learned the difference between Sky's hungry cry, wet cry, and tired cry. She took lots of cell phone photos of her beautiful baby to share with her and Aaron's mom, and anyone else who was interested. She flashed pictures before an unresponsive Aaron, describing each change and special event, hoping for something – anything to let her know he understood.

Anna's mom, Becky, flew in from California to help out. She cuddled and fed her new granddaughter, giving Anna a chance to catch up on some much-needed rest. Becky had only a week before she had to return home. A quick visit to Aaron's hospital room left her feeling sorry for her daughter and her lost love. She suggested ever so gently that it might be better for all if Anna agreed to let Aaron go.

Aaron's mom, Sky, arrived; bring gifts for her new grandchild and namesake. A visit to the hospital room where her son lay lifeless overshadowed the bundle of joy she came to welcome into the world. Sky reluctantly agreed with Anna's mother. It was difficult for them to understand why, after all this time, she wouldn't let him go. His body had been through major trauma, and Sky was sure her son would not want to live under the circumstances. His whole life he had been vibrant and full of love. The motionless body in the bed looked like her son but, she was certain, if he couldn't open his eyes to see his beautiful new daughter, he was not there.

Aaron's mother said the words Anna could not bear to hear. "I think you should unplug him. His heart beats because of a machine, not because he is filled with life."

Anna understood what they were saying – why they were saying it, but she wasn't ready to let go. She wasn't ready to give up.

The moms' visits were filled with joy and sadness, highs and lows. Tear-filled goodbyes held promises that they would learn how to Skype, so they could share in every change and milestone in their granddaughter's life. Anna was grateful they came, but relieved when they left. She didn't want to talk or think about unplugging the father of her child, the love of her life.

\*      \*      \*      \*      \*

The date arrived for Priscilla to visit Aaron's bedside. Anna was apprehensive. She asked Terri if she'd watch Sky for a while so that she could go to the hospital and visit Aaron. Terri was happy to have Sky all to herself. She brought a surprise for her new little niece. Terry couldn't resist the furry brown, stuffed coyote she saw in the store window. She had to buy it for the new addition to her world. It was a funny coincidence that Anna bought the same little stuffed coyote for Sky just the day before.

Anna placed them side by side in the crib. "I think these cute, little, twin coyotes belong in this room. I'm sure they'll be Sky's favorites."

\*      \*      \*      \*      \*

Anna left for the hospital to visit Aaron. Her visits were sporadic since Sky was born, but now she felt like her schedule was more predictable. Her daily routine included a hospital visit, just as it had before Sky was born. When Anna arrived at Aaron's room, Priscilla was sitting by his bed with her eyes closed.

The floor nurse walked by and whispered to Anna, "She said she was a friend of the family."

Anna smiled and shook her head, acknowledging her approval. She sat in a chair against the wall, so she wouldn't interfere with whatever it was Priscilla was doing. Priscilla didn't move, she just sat there silently holding Aaron's hand.

After what seemed to be a very long time, she signaled Anna to come closer. "Why don't you hold his other hand and talk to him."

Anna had many conversations with Aaron over the months with no reaction, but she did what Priscilla asked.

"Hi, Aaron, Sky is with Terri today. Our baby girl is changing every day. People say she looks like me but has your coloring."

Anna looked at Priscilla searching for more direction.

All Priscilla said was, "Please continue."

Anna returned her attention to Aaron. "The baby's room is finished. Bill and Terri helped me, and it's perfect."

Priscilla sat up straight in the chair and said loudly, "No heat! No heat!"

Then she settled back in her chair once again.

Anna was surprised. "What was that?" she asked.

Priscilla looked up. "Aaron wants you to know there is no heat in the little bedroom. It needs to be fixed. He loves you both very much."

That's all she said. It was all over quickly.

Priscilla stood and looked at Anna with a seemingly pleased smile. "He's still here. Not strong enough to come back completely, but still here."

They walked out of the room arm in arm. Anna was still not sure the message was right. Although disappointed, she was grateful Priscilla attempted to connect to him.

She, too, believed Aaron was still there. "Thank you so much. I'll check the heat in the little bedroom, but I don't think there's a problem."

Priscilla smiled. "Okay, dear, come see me again if you like. You have beautiful energy and so does your husband."

Anna asked how much she owed her for her time.

Priscilla lowered her head. "No charge this time. If you need me again I'll ask you for twenty-five dollars for my time and for a twenty-five-dollar donation to the food pantry."

That seemed fair to Anna, but she was quite sure she wouldn't need Priscilla again. It was silly for her to think a psychic could help.

Anna sent a text to Terri letting her know she was on the way home. Terri was hoping she would have more time with Sky. All Sky did was sleep while her mother was gone, and Terri was hoping for a kiss and a cuddle. When she returned Anna decided to tell Terri about Priscilla's visit with Aaron.

As she suspected Terri was amused. "Did you really think a psychic could talk to Aaron?"

Anna, feeling a little silly, said, "Well, I thought it was worth a shot. The only thing she could tell me is Aaron wanted me to know Sky's room needs heat, and he loves us both."

Terri raised her eyebrows. "You know, I kept Sky in the bassinet down here, because her room was so cold. I even checked the vents to make sure they were open. Really, I'm not kidding, it's freezing up there."

Terri followed Anna upstairs to Sky's room. It was cold - very cold. Anna decided to call her furnace guy, so that he could check it out. Meanwhile, she would keep the bassinet in her bedroom where it was warm.

"What do think about that, Terri?" she asked.

Terri laughed. "I don't know what to think. It's kind of creepy."

Anna was not surprised that Terri was still resistant to the thought that Aaron was sending messages but, it didn't matter, she was sure he was.

\*    \*    \*    \*    \*

Life was full and busy. Over the years following Sky's birth, Anna became editor of the newspaper. She took over for Terri who accepted an editorial position with a magazine. The added responsibility was a welcomed challenge for Anna, and a bonus was the flexible schedule that working for a weekly newspaper offered. She could work from home most days and easily meet all the needs of her growing daughter.

Anna chronicled each of Sky's achievements as she grew; sitting up by herself, crawling, her first tooth, first step, her first word, and her first day of school. As she got older Sky looked more like Anna but had Aaron's dark hair and eyes. Anna saw flashes of Aaron's smile from time to time when Sky laughed. Bill was her rock and became Sky's surrogate dad. He changed diapers, babysat, and played Santa. Sky became very attached to Uncle Bill, and it was apparent that he loved her, too.

Hospital visits with Sky were few and far between. The tubes and monitors frightened her, and she could not connect to the lifeless body in the bed named Daddy.

At five she was beautiful, smart, and playful. Auntie Terri and Uncle Bill were her favorites, and she loved them both. Uncle Bill introduced Sky to a new member of the family; a black, lab puppy. Anna's beloved Bud passed away when he was fourteen. It had been several years since, but Anna was not ready to fill his place until now. She missed her Bud; for so long he had filled the roll of her loyal companion. Bill convinced her that Sky was at the perfect age for a new puppy.

Tucked in Bill's arms was a little guy that looked just like Bud did when Aaron brought him home. His fur was soft and shiny, reminding Anna of black, patent leather.

Bill squatted down and held the puppy so that Sky could pat his head. "What do you think we should call him?" he asked.

Sky thought for a moment. With a quick, assured move of her head she said, "I think we should call him Blackie."

Bill glanced at Anna and received a smiled of approval.

"Blackie it is then," he said, confirming her choice.

They celebrated the new family member with a mug of hot chocolate covered with floating tufts of whipped cream.

Right from the start Blackie loved Sky as much as she loved him. The old boys sniffed the newcomer but were apparently indifferent to his arrival. Anna was pleased with her new boy and the unmistakable connection he and Sky had from the moment they met.

Sky asked if she could take Blackie outside for a little while before supper.

Anna agreed, yelling from the window, "Don't go far; we are going to eat in ten minutes!"

Sky picked Blackie up holding him around his belly, allowing his hind quarter to swing back and forth as she walked around the back yard.

Anna tapped on the window. "Put him down and let him investigate the yard."

The older boys curled up on the rug, only lifting their ears slightly when they heard Anna's tapping. Bill pitched in setting the table while Anna rounded up bowls and serving spoons.

Sky was outside with Blackie for about fifteen minutes when Anna called her in for dinner, but neither she nor the puppy could be seen.

Anna felt a pang in the pit of her stomach. "Bill, I don't see Sky or the puppy anywhere."

She opened the back door and call out, but there was no answer. Anna heard the familiar voice echo in her ears.

She hadn't heard it in a long time, but it was unmistakable.

"Go to the pond, now! Go now!"

Anna cried out, "Oh, no, Bill, the pond!"

The pond was about four hundred feet behind the barn and could not be seen from the house. Anna ran outside, bounding in the direction of the pond. Bill and the boys followed quickly behind. Floating on the edge of the water Anna could see Sky's motionless body. Bill strode passed Anna, wading waist deep into the water, lifting Sky's lifeless form. She hung from his arms like a wet, rag doll. Gently he placed her on the grass and began CPR.

Anna fell to her knees holding her breath, searching for a change - searching for a sign of life. It seemed like forever but, finally, Sky began to cough, choking up water. She opened her eyes gasping for breath. Bill and Anna wrapped their arms around Sky and each other, thanking God that she was alive. The puppy peeked out of the tall grass as the boys circled around and nudged him into the open. At that moment, they knew the whole family was safe.

The pediatrician checked Sky from head to toe and said the words they were praying to hear. "She is perfect. You can take her home."

Speaking sternly the doctor turned to Sky and said, "Now, Sky, you stay away from that pond unless Mommy or Daddy is with you, understand?"

Sky moved her head slowly in agreement. "I thought my puppy, Blackie, was in the water. He ran ahead of me, and I couldn't see him. I fell over a log and couldn't get up."

Anna was uncomfortable knowing how close she had come to losing her daughter. She watched with relief as Bill took Sky's hand and led her out of the doctor's office to the car. Anna thanked the doctor and joined her two sidekicks outside.

"Can we get an ice cream?" Sky asked.

Bill didn't hesitate. "I think that can be arranged. Let's get ice cream all around."

Anna smiled in agreement. An ice cream celebration seemed appropriate.

After the celebration, they were homeward bound. Anna took Sky up to bed, read her a story, and hugged her good night. Walking down the stairs she flashed Bill a smile. "She's asleep now, asleep and safe."

Anna closed her eyes releasing a long exhale. "Bill, I don't know what I would have done if I lost her. I'm so glad you were here today. You always seem to know what to do. Thank you."

Bill walked over to Anna and wrapped his arms around her. She relaxed, leaning into his strong, muscular body and, for one minute - for just one minute, she let herself go. He reached down and drew her face to his, pressing his lips softly against hers. Her body responded with a stirring she hadn't felt in many years. The kiss deepened as their bodies pressed closer. Anna caught herself wanting - needing more, but instead she pushed him away.

"This is wrong, Bill. I can't."

Bill straightened awkwardly, releasing her immediately. "Anna, I love you. You must know that I've loved you for a very long time. When are you going to let go of Aaron? You know I love Sky as if she were my own."

Anna felt her anger rising. "I know you think Aaron is dead, but he's not dead! Aaron is not dead! He told me where to find Sky today. I won't kill him!"

She felt angry at herself for letting go, even for just a moment. "I know you don't understand, but he tells me things. How can you understand? I don't understand. I can't unplug him."

Bill took a deep breath, turned, and headed toward the door. "I love you. I'm here. He is in a hospital bed hooked up to machines. That's the only reason he is breathing. You need to let him go, if not for yourself, for Sky."

Anna's body was shaking as she alternated between anger and sadness. She watched Bill leave, closing the door behind him with a bang.

Bill stopped coming by to check on Anna and Sky. They only saw him occasionally over the next few weeks. The visits were short, a hug for Sky, a pat for the boys, sometimes a coffee and a bagel for her.

"Just checking to see if you need anything," he would say. Bill was different - distant. Anna didn't blame him, but she missed him. The memory of their kiss lingered, but now he seemed more like a concerned neighbor not the Bill she had grown so dependent on, the man she needed and wanted in her life.

*    *    *    *    *

There had been no contact between Pricilla and Anna since the visit to the hospital. But Anna could think of nothing else. Sitting at the computer she began a search to find Priscilla's website, but nothing came up. Continuing her search, she came across an article about a woman claiming to be a psychic, who was under investigation for tax evasion. The name was Priscilla Preston. Anna was sure it was the same Priscilla.

Calling Sky, she grabbed their jackets and her handbag. "Sky, let's go for a ride. I have to talk to someone."

Sky was happy to go for a ride with Mommy and took everything she needed for the trip; her iPad, her forest ranger doll, and her two little coyotes. She placed her treasures carefully in her backpack and followed her mother out the door. Anna found the house easily but wasn't sure if Priscilla still lived there. When she pulled into the driveway she could see the same wicker furniture, slightly faded, but the same. A car was parked in the driveway, and that made her think that Priscilla was still living there. Getting out of the car she told Sky she would be just a minute. As she approached the house, Priscilla opened the front door and waived her in. Sky hopped out of the car and followed her mother into the house.

Priscilla hugged Anna. "This must be Sky."

Anna was a little surprised. She didn't recall mentioning Sky's name in their conversations.

She guided Anna and Sky to her kitchen table. "Please sit down. Aaron is watching over you both. He isn't always strong enough to communicate with you, but most of the time he can connect with me."

Anna was skeptical. "What does he say to you?"

Priscilla's eyes were piercing. "He mostly wants to come back to you and Sky, but his body is too weak."

Anna felt confused. "Is there anything I can do to help him come back?"

Priscilla put the palms of her hands together and placed them under her chin, as if praying. "Well, dear, that is out of your hands. There is a power greater than ours that determines these things."

Anna could feel her anger rising. "Then why - why do I hear from him at all? Why do you hear from him?"

Priscilla took a deep breath and began to speak but was interrupted.

Sky yanked on Anna's sleeve. "Mommy, Daddy talks to me, too. He told me not to go near the pond."

Anna turned to Sky. "What did you say, Sky? Daddy speaks to you?"

Sky shook her head. "Not all the time, but sometimes. I know it's Daddy because he says so. One time I was standing on the bureau drawer trying to reach my iPad and he told me to get off fast. The bureau almost tipped over."

"Sometimes children are more open to these things," explained Priscilla with a warm smile.

Anna reached out for Sky's hand. "I don't know where to go with this. I want to believe it, all of it, but what good does any of this do? We have to go but, first, I'd like to know why your website has been taken down. I read something about tax evasion."

The lines in Priscilla's brow deepened. "Dear, there are always people who do not believe and who want to stop what they don't understand. I have to be more careful about how I report my income, that's all."

Anna put twenty-five dollars on the table. "I'll give the same amount to our local food pantry. Thank you for your time, Priscilla."

On the drive home Sky played quietly in the back seat as Anna tried to sort out what she had just heard. Calling Terri, she asked if she could stop by for a minute. She needed to talk to someone.

Over tea, Terri listened quietly as Anna described her visit with Priscilla.

Terri thought for a moment. "I think she's playing with you. Did she charge you for the time?"

Sky was in the other room watching her favorite TV show, which made Anna feel more comfortable talking about the messages from Aaron. One of the big questions she had was why Sky hadn't told her that she heard Aaron's voice. Had she listened to a discussion between Anna and Bill? Did the subject come up when Sky was in the room, and she absorbed the details as children sometimes do? Terri listened without response. Anna grew silent.

Terri asked, "Why do you need this to be true? Why are you trying to keep Aaron alive? He died six years ago. Why can't you let him go?"

Anna looked up. "I know you don't believe me, but I know I hear him. He is not dead; at least I don't think he is. Do you think this is easy for me? I miss him so much, and I'm so angry with him. He left me here alone. He didn't die, and he didn't live. I can't go forward with my life, because I'm tied to a man who isn't alive and isn't dead. Except for Sky, my life is in a coma just as much as his!"

Terri stood up, walked around the table, and put her arms around Anna as her anger turned to tears as it so often did.

"Let's have a glass of wine," Terri suggested.

Anna was ready to leave. "No, I have to get Sky home. Thank you for listening. I'll call you later."

Anna grabbed a tissue, wiped her nose and called Sky.

As the days passed Anna decided to stop thinking about her visit with Priscilla, and she didn't want to again hear Terri's opinion that Aaron was dead. There were too many questions and no answers. She was frustrated, because the people she loved most did not understand or believe what she was saying. She wasn't sure about Sky's story either. Anna kept waiting for a sign, but none came. Her visits to the hospital remained the same; beep, beep, beep was the only sound that filled the room.

\*     \*     \*     \*     \*

It was Saturday and Sky was upstairs playing princess when a storm warning flashed across the TV screen. From the looks of the sky the storm was brewing to the north. Days were getting shorter, and the fall weather was reflected in the changing colors of the trees. There was a flash of lightening and a bang of thunder that sent Sky scurrying downstairs to cuddle with her mother. The boys gathered around.

Anna comforted Sky. "I have a flashlight and candles, in case we lose electricity, and a new book we can read together. Mr. and Mrs. Coyote are right here with us. We are safe, and the storm will be over soon."

Another flash of lighting and several booms rang out. The house went dark and hail began to ping and scratch against the windows. The sky lit up again and again, as the wind took leaves off the trees and bounced anything that wasn't secured, ending finally in sudden silence.

"Okay, Sky, it's bedtime." Anna held her hand out to guide Sky to bed, using the flashlight to light their way.

"Can I sleep with you tonight, Mommy?"

Anna smiled. "Yes, we can cuddle. Tomorrow I'll make us blueberry pancakes for breakfast."

"Will Uncle Bill have pancakes with us too?" Sky asked. The lights flickered on, and the TV set began a slow rebooted.

"Okay, Sky, we're all lit up now, but you can still sleep with me tonight. We'll do pancakes in the morning as we planned, just you and me."

Anna tucked Sky into bed, placing her little coyotes on each side, promising she wouldn't be long. As she went downstairs to clean up for the night, her phone buzzed on the counter. She was hoping it was Bill.

"Hello, is this Mrs. Rogers?"

Anna didn't recognize the voice. "Yes, this is Mrs. Rogers. Who is this?"

"This is, Mrs. Kyotee, the floor nurse at Memorial Hospital. Your husband just opened his eyes. We would like you to come in as soon as possible."

It took Anna a moment to fully understand what she just heard.

Anna began to shake. "Did you say my husband opened his eyes? Yes, I'll be there right away."

Immediately she called Terri and told her about the call from the hospital and asked if she would stay with Sky.

Terri hesitated for a second, trying to understand what Anna had just said. "He's opened his eyes? Of course, I'm on my way."

When Anna arrived at the hospital she went directly to Aaron's room. It buzzed with activity as the hospital team busily conducted tests. There hadn't been this much activity in his room for a long time.

One of the doctors came to her side and held out his hand. "I'm happy you were able to come so quickly, Mrs. Rogers. There have been some dramatic changes in your husband's condition. During the storm, the hospital was hit by lightning, which created a power surge and disrupted our medical equipment. We're going to be running more tests but, it seems, as a result, your husband is awake. His eyes are open, and his pupils are responsive. We don't know how much brain damage he has sustained as yet - well, if any. That's what we'll be looking at over the next couple of weeks. But we would like you to talk to him and see if he responds."

Anna walked toward the bed as she had so many times before. It had been six years; six years of beep, beep, beep, six years of tubes, and tests, and monitors, six years of seizures and infections. But this time was different. Aaron lay motionless, but his eyes were open and, as she approached, she could see recognition in his eyes. She reached down and touched his hand. Slowly his fingers wrapped around hers. Tears ran down her face and, as she stood over him, Aaron slowly smiled.

Leaning down, she kissed his forehead and whispered softly. "Welcome back, my love. I've been waiting for you."

The doctor was pleased. "This is good. We'll do more testing and put a plan together for physical therapy. I want to caution you though, this may not last, and there could be other complications. We'll take it one step at a time."

Anna understood that life had taken another turn. Sky had her daddy back, she had her husband back and, as far as she was concerned, it was all good.

\* \* \* \* \*

As each day passed Aaron improved a little bit more. He was sitting up, and his voice was getting stronger. Although he didn't recall the accident, and there were other gaps in his memory, Anna had faith everything would eventually come back to him. Soon she could take him home. There were a few things she had to arrange before that could happen. He needed a hospital bed on the first floor and some other accommodations made in the bathroom, but that would not be difficult. She was also taking another big step. For the first time since Aaron opened his eyes, she was going to bring Sky to the hospital to see her Daddy.

\* \* \* \* \*

Sky was not happy about going to the hospital. It was a long time since her last visit, and she was afraid of the man lying in the hospital bed who was called Daddy. Sky was dawdling as much as possible in hopes that her mother would not make her go. Uncle Bill stopped by unexpectedly.

Excited, Sky ran to him wrapping her arms around his legs.

"I miss you. Where have you been, Uncle Bill?"

Anna agreed. "Yes, Bill, we have missed you. We're going to see Aaron today. I'm sure Terri has told you he's awake."

Aaron struggled to smile. "Yes, I know. Terri told me everything."

He knew Aaron was getting stronger, had some memory lapses, and was having headaches.

"Terri said Aaron is having impulse control and anger issues. Are you sure it's safe to bring him home?"

Anna thought for a moment. "Yes, all of that is true, but this is going to take time. He has medication to help him and physical therapy will continue until he gets stronger. A therapist is scheduled to come to the house twice a week. The doctors have assured me this is the best course for his recovery. He needs to be in his home with everything – with us."

Sky was silently listening. "Uncle Bill, will you come with us to see my daddy? I'm scared."

Anna looked at the two of them. Bill was holding Sky, her arm wrapped around his neck. Anna knew this is what Sky had been missing.

She had to agree. "Yes, Uncle Bill, why don't you come with us? You can see Daddy, too. It's been a long time."

Bill hesitated but, as Sky hugged him a little tighter, he agreed to go with them. They headed for the car, Bill carrying Sky under his arm like a sack of potatoes, while she giggled and waived her arms in the air all the way.

When they arrived at the hospital Sky hesitated before getting out of the car. Anna held out her hand to help her daughter take the next big step in her life; meeting her father. When they entered the hospital room they saw Aaron sitting in a wheelchair with a blanket neatly arranged across his legs. His muscles had atrophied from so many years in a coma but, with the physical therapy sessions, he was already seeing progress. Recovery was slow but steady.

Aaron smiled when he saw his visitors. "Bill, it's good to see you."

Holding out his arms, he welcomed his daughter. "Hi, Sky, come see Daddy."

Sky ducked behind Bill's legs, clutching him tightly.

Again, Aaron spoke to Sky. "Come see Daddy, Sky. I would like to give you a hug."

Sky hung on to Bill, burying her head in his legs. Anna was not surprised by Sky's response. She knew him as Daddy, but he was a stranger to her.

Bill took Sky's hand and led her to Aaron's side. "Sky, your Daddy is feeling better and wants to give you a hug."

Sky stood in front of the wheelchair with her fingers in her mouth. Swaying back and forth she mumbled, "Hi, Daddy."

Aaron stretched his arms out closer to her. "Sky, come give Daddy a hug. You are such a big girl."

Sky turned and ran to her mother.

Anna looked at Aaron and said, "I think we can come back again tomorrow. Maybe Sky can bring Daddy a drawing for his wall."

"That sounds like a good idea," said a nurse who was observing the scene.

Bill approached Aaron and placed his hand on his shoulder. "It's good to see you, my friend. Welcome back."

Aaron's brow tightened and his eyes narrowed, as he glanced back and forth from Bill to Anna. Sky ran into the hall calling for Uncle Bill. Bill followed, picking her up and hugging her close.

Anna kissed Aaron on his forehead. "Don't worry; Sky will need a little time to get to know you. Be patient; she's just a little girl."

Aaron looked into Anna's eyes. "How long did it take her to get to know Bill?"

Anna stepped back, took a deep breath, and reminded herself what the doctor warned her about. With Aaron's type of brain injury there could be personality changes. He may have trouble adjusting to his environment, very probably bouts of depression, and unexpected outbursts of anger. He could have any combination or every combination, only time would tell.

She stayed focused. "We'll be back tomorrow. You rest. I think Sky is excited about making you a picture for your wall."

Aaron looked down at his feet. "Yes, I'm looking forward to tomorrow, too."

*    *    *    *    *

The trip home was filled with Sky's questions about Daddy's wheelchair. She wanted to know how long Daddy lived at the hospital and why he had been sleeping for so long. Bill patiently answered her questions. Anna knew that they had just had a preview of how Aaron's emotions may play out. He was coming home soon, and there were so many things they would have to find out as they went along. They told her he would get physically stronger but, from what she had just seen, she was more worried about his mental and emotional health.

Anna put Sky to bed reminding her that they would decide on a picture for Daddy's wall in the morning. The boys stayed with Sky, and Anna went downstairs to thank Bill for taking them to the hospital.

"I think it's going to take Sky a while to warm up to Aaron," Bill said breaking the silence.

"Yes," agreed Anna, "to her, he is a stranger named Daddy. She's a stranger to him, too. Bill, Sky loves you. I'm worried that she might not love Aaron in the same way?"

Bill walked over and sat down beside her. "Look, Aaron has a long way to go. I'll be here for you and Sky for as long as you need me."

Anna stiffened. "I don't know if Aaron can handle how close you and Sky have become. I think your relationship with her threatens their relationship and may get in the way of their bonding. It's not going to be easy for him to fill your shoes."

Bill grew silent for a moment. "Are you saying you want me to stay away?"

Anna spoke carefully. "I don't want you to stay away, but I think they will need time together without you. Sky has to get to know her daddy."

Bill stood up, holding back what he really wanted to say. Anna saw the sadness in his eyes.

Walking to the door, he stopped. "Goodbye, Anna. Please say goodbye to Sky for me."

Anna watched as he moved down the walkway, got into his car and drove away. Her heart was aching. When she lost Aaron six years ago, Bill was the one who helped her heal. Now she had lost him, too. She knew Sky would be looking for her Uncle Bill. Anna also knew she had to make Aaron the most important person in their lives. It would take time, but she felt they could do it. She brushed back her tears, shut off the lights, and wet upstairs to bed.

*    *    *    *    *

It took several months of hard work before Aaron was strong enough to walk with only a cane. He was still experiencing frequent migraines and fighting periods of depression. Medication lessened the frequency of his headaches, but their intensity was still debilitating. Slowly his appetite returned, and his muscle tone was improving. He was becoming stronger overall.

The day he went home was a mix of excitement and apprehension for Anna. The house was ready. His hospital bed was in place in the corner of the living room, and the first-floor bathroom was now handicap accessible. Depending on his strength and pain level, he alternately used a cane or a walker. Sometimes the wheelchair was his choice for the day as a result of his ever-present balance issues.

Aaron could navigate the kitchen with little assistance, and his living space was located in the heart of the household.

Sky did little to acknowledge the changes in her home and her family life. She skipped in and out of the house as if everything was exactly as it had been. She escaped to her bedroom or the backyard with the boys whenever she felt uncomfortable. Often Sky asked for permission to eat at a friend's house, sometimes staying overnight. Her attention was focused on her school assignments, teachers, and her friends. She stopped asking for Uncle Bill, but Anna knew Sky missed him, and so did she.

The school bus arrived at the end of the driveway at 7:00 A.M. and returned at 3:30 P.M. The boys greeted Sky every afternoon and walked with her to the house. Anna was working mostly from home. It was important that she be available if Aaron needed help and for her to be there when Sky got off the school bus. The mud room worked perfectly as her home office. The structure of their life had changed but, with the adjustments they made, it seemed to be working efficiently.

In addition to physical therapy, Aaron was seeing a counselor for depression. Anna began counseling as well. The changes in her life left her feeling anxious and hypervigilant. She didn't want to make a mistake and needed help in guiding Sky. Aaron's meds were changed often. Each time she hoped they found the magic pill that would soothe his anger and calm his pain. More frequently than not a change led to different side effects, but side effects nevertheless. The schedule of doctors' appointments was ongoing and ever-changing. Although Aaron looked the same physically, all he had been through and was going through had changed him. Anna missed his kindness, his patience, his sense of humor. She missed the sound of his laughter and sight of his dimple flashing as he smiled. He was angry most of the time: angry his body didn't move the way he wanted it to, angry he didn't feel well and was in pain, and angry his wife and daughter felt like distant strangers.

\*     \*     \*     \*     \*

Life was a rollercoaster ride for the family. They ate meals together, struggling to find conversation that wasn't about Aaron's health or his most recent doctor's appointment. Uncle Bill was never mentioned. Sky knew talk of Uncle Bill upset her mother and made her father angry.

The White Mountains called to Aaron every day. He could see Mount Washington from the backyard. The majestic beauty of the mountains soothed him. Watching the movement of the trees as they swayed in the breeze was hypnotic and brought him peace. In his first weeks at home, he mastered maneuvering his wheelchair to his workshop in the barn. He loved the smell, feel, and tones of the wood. Ever since he was a young boy he naturally gravitated towards woodworking and had an artist's touch; carving beautiful creations from a fallen branch or tree stump. He worked meticulously, releasing the vision he saw in each piece. Those were the only moments he felt whole and almost pain free.

Anna longed for the closeness they once had. The only time they touched was when he needed her helped getting dressed. She felt more like an aide than a wife. Aaron often told her he appreciated what she did for him but, to her, he always sounded like a polite stranger. Anna wondered if he would ever be able to come to their bed. He remained distant and never reached out for her.

Sky witnessed several outbursts. Aaron's emotions boiled over easily when his body wouldn't move the way he wanted it to or when a migraine took his breath away. It was difficult for Anna to endure his mood swings, but they were devastating for their seven-year-old daughter.

When the doctor asked how they were doing, all Anna could say was, "Fine."

She didn't know how to talk about her needs. She felt selfish thinking about herself when she saw her husband in such pain. Every time a new medication was added or stopped, Aaron had a reaction. Nothing seemed to alleviate his pain. His balance was good some days, but other days sitting in his wheelchair was challenging. Anna hoped that one day they would rekindle their passion, but he was not the man she once felt passion for.

The doctor assured her she was doing everything possible to help him heal. Physical therapy was making him stronger and, in time, they would find the right combination of medications so he could sustain a more normal life. The doctor could not guarantee that she would have the old Aaron back, but she would have a version of him. With each episode, each change in medication, the doctor reminded her that she needed to be patient.

Anna was struggling; angry with Aaron one minute and feeling sorry for him the next. She didn't want to share a life with a version of Aaron, she wanted the Aaron she fell in love with back. He had been home for months with little improvement. She watched him as he struggled with pain and depression, but was unable to help. Sky stayed away from her father as much as she could, and it appeared that he stopped trying to win her love. The only time he seemed at peace was when he was in his workshop in the barn.

$$* \quad * \quad * \quad * \quad *$$

Sky and Anna went to the store and left Aaron sleeping soundly on his bed in the living room. When he woke up he read the note Anna left saying they wouldn't be long. He moved slowly to his desk holding his head steady to keep the dizziness at bay, and being careful so he wouldn't fall again. The last time he fell he was alone, and it caused a major setback. Anna wouldn't leave him alone for weeks after. She was just again beginning to get comfortable, only taking short jaunts while leaving him on his own. He hated that he was so dependent on her.

The doorbell rang.

This morning, like so many other mornings, he didn't have enough strength to stand and walk to the door, so he yelled, "Come on in!"

When the door opened he could see a large woman with long salt and pepper hair, dressed in a colorful kaftan.

As she entered, in a loud voice, she said, "How are you, Aaron?"

Pulling himself to his feet with the help of his cane he stood as straight as his body would allow. "What are you doing here?"

"You know why I'm here. You were not supposed to return. Why did you come back?"

Aaron looked at the floor, head bowed. "There is something I have to do for Sky. It's none of your business. I'm handling this, and I don't appreciate your interference. Now get out of here, and don't come back."

The woman turned sharply to leave.

Reaching out to close the door behind her she looked over her shoulder at Aaron. "You know you do not belong here."

She raised her hand and pointed her finger directly at him. "Fix this!"

Pain shot through Aaron's head. Using his cane, he pushed the desk chair out of the way so he could get to his pills. He needed to stop the pain. Two pills - no, four pills would be better - work faster. He choked them down waiting - wanting quick relief. Just before Anna and Sky returned home, his pain became bearable.

After putting the groceries away Anna and Sky went into the garden. Sky happily helped her mother deadhead the flowers and water the plants. Sky's constant companion, Blackie, stayed close by. Anna was relieved that Aaron spent some time by himself and remained accident free. She was leaving him for only short periods of time after the scare from his last fall. This was a good sign; so far, so good.

From the garden Anna could hear the buzz of the cell phone inside the house. Through the window she could see Aaron, who had just returned from his workshop, sitting in front of the computer. He reached out, grabbed for his cane, and struggled to his feet.

The movement from sitting to standing made him dizzy. A new medication often added unforeseen side effects. His migraine meds had just been changed and, although the duration of his headaches had decreased, his dizziness was intensifying. In addition, he began experiencing a persistent radiating pain between his eyes that affected his vision. Wanting fast relief from the pain, he often took a double dose of his medication.

The dizziness caused him to lose his balance and, tipping slightly to one side, he threw his arms out to stop from falling, sending the laptop crashing to the floor. Anna heard the crash and ran into the house.

"What happened?" was all she said, sending Aaron into a tirade.

He was on the floor with the laptop in pieces beside him. Sky ran in following her mother and stopped short when she saw Daddy flailing on the floor.

Immediately Anna stooped down to helped Aaron back to the chair. Angry, he pushed her away, slamming her body against the wall.

Sky shouted, "Daddy, why are you hurting Mommy?"

Aaron covered his face with his hands, but said nothing.

Anna reached out to comfort her daughter. "Sky, it was an accident. Daddy didn't mean it; he just lost his balance."

Sky was witness to Aaron's anger before. There were many harsh words and glances between Mommy and Daddy. She rarely went near her father, afraid he would lash out at her, too.

"I hate you! I want Uncle Bill back. Why don't you go back to the hospital to live!" She ran up the stairs to her bedroom, slamming the door behind her.

"Are you going to let her talk to me like that?" Aaron growled.

Anna, holding a painful shoulder, was trying to understand what had just happened."I'll talk to her, Aaron. All of this has been hard on her."

"Hard on her!" he bellowed, "How do you think I feel? I'm in constant pain, my body doesn't work, and my wife and daughter are in love with another man!"

Anna couldn't believe what Aaron said. "I'm going to call the doctor and make an appointment for you. I think your meds need to be changed again."

Aaron threw his cane on the floor and grabbed for his pills. Walking outside, Anna took her phone into the garden and dialed Bill; something she hadn't done in almost a year. She wasn't sure what she was going to say, she just needed to hear his voice. When the call connected she got his recorded message. His voice sounded warm and comforting which only made her miss him more. His message was short, but enough to make her feel better. She hung up. Anna felt it was wrong to lean on him, especially now.

Her shoulder was throbbing from being slammed into the wall. Although Anna knew Aaron didn't mean to hurt her, his outbursts and erratic behavior were getting worse. The doctor warned her time and time again, that with his type of brain injury, it would take time to find the right balance of meds to manage his pain and emotional ups and downs. They really didn't know what, if anything, would work. It was wait and see, trial and error. All Anna knew for sure was that life was difficult for Sky and her, and there was no relief in sight. She longed for Bill's strong presence, even disposition, and caring ways. Hearing his voice message made her miss him even more. She stayed outside until her tears dried, but her longing to feel Bill's arms around her didn't fade.

Anna righted the chair and picked up the pieces of the computer. Luckily, when she turned it on, it rebooted. The computer case was banged up, but the pieces on the floor were from a desk lamp that got knocked over as Aaron struggled to keep his balance.

He was sitting in the kitchen. "Are you all right? I didn't mean to hurt you. My head hurts. You're right, my meds aren't working."

Anna knew he was struggling. "It will be okay. Do you need help going to bed before I go upstairs?"

As she walked into the kitchen she could see that Aaron was sitting in his wheelchair, holding his head in his hands. She walked behind him and rested her hand on his shoulder. It was the extent of their closeness. It was all she had to give and all he would allow.

Aaron lowered his head. "I'm fine. I can manage. Good night."

Anna knew that was the best he could do.

*     *     *     *     *

After one of his episodes everyone went about their day as if nothing happened. Anna took aspirin for her still aching shoulder, everything on the desk was back in place, and Sky skipped happily to the school bus stop, followed by the boys.

Aaron flipped through the newspaper curious about upcoming events for the White Mountain National Forest, but could find nothing. He moved to the computer and searched for a website that would give him the schedule he was looking for. He knew that Bill replaced him as Forest Supervisor after the accident. Thinking about it, his anger again began to rise. It was another thing he had lost to the man that took the love of his wife and daughter away from him. The buzz of the cell phone broke the early morning silence. Aaron reached out and answered the phone quickly.

"Hello." The voice was familiar. "This is Ted. How the heck are you, Aaron?"

It was the first time Ted spoke to his old friend, Aaron, since the accident. Bill gave him updates from time to time, but he wanted to speak to Aaron himself. Ted stopped visiting the hospital after the first year but, when he heard how well Aaron was doing and the miraculous recovery, he wanted to reconnect.

Aaron was happy to hear from him. "I'm good. I still have some physical limitations, so I'm not ready to go back to work yet. The docs are still trying to get my headaches under control. My goal is to get back to my old job by the end of the year. So, I'm doing really well. I'm good."

Ted didn't know for sure if Aaron was up to an outing, but thought it couldn't hurt to ask. "I'm happy to hear you're doing better. I was thinking, how about I pick you up one day next week, let's say Tuesday. You can come to the Ranger Station and say hi to all the guys. We'll give you an update on everything that's going on. What do you think?"

After what seemed like a long silence, Aaron agreed. He hadn't been back to the station since the accident. He wasn't sure if he had the energy, but decided to accept the invitation.

There wasn't much Aaron looked forward to anymore, but the thought of visiting the Ranger Station was beginning to feel good to him. He wanted to show them how well he was doing, and that he was working on going back to his old job. He was determined to again be Forest Supervisor. Aaron lost time and was still struggling, but he was unwavering in his goal and wasn't ready to give up. He felt like he was at war and this was a battle he was not willing to lose.

*     *     *     *     *

When Tuesday morning came around Ted arrived bringing coffee and donuts. Anna was happy to see him and was pleased that Aaron seemed excited about the outing. This was the first time he'd done anything except go to doctor's appointments. Sky was in school and that would give her some badly needed alone time. Anna helped Aaron get ready, knowing he was looking forward to seeing everyone, but it was apparent to her he was also apprehensive. This was the first time he was going out without her. She wanted to give Ted instructions but, knew if she did, she would embarrass Aaron and make him angry. She refrained.

Aaron's goal for the visit was to show them all how well he was doing. He felt like the same man inside. His body didn't work the way it once did, but there was no reason they had to know. He didn't want anyone to feel sorry for him, even though at times he felt sorry for himself.

As a passenger in Ted's truck Aaron thought about when he was the one in the driver's seat. Ted tried to keep the conversation moving, but Aaron just shook his head and said "Yes" or "No" at the appropriate time. It was apparent to Ted that Aaron's thoughts were somewhere else, and he was barely listening.

Being in the truck brought back memories for Aaron. Since he awoke from the coma he was living someone else's life in a body that no longer worked. All of his outings were from the house to the hospital for more testing or to the doctor's office, always with Anna as his support system. He never drove. The ride to the Ranger Station was a welcome break, but he wanted to be the one in the driver's seat. He hated being treated like an invalid. He hated feeling like an invalid. He hated that he had to depend on other people to survive.

Arriving at their destination, Ted grabbed Aaron's cane from the back seat and walked around the truck to give him a hand getting out. He warned him the step was high. Aaron didn't want Ted's help. He pulled the cane from Ted's hand and threw it to the ground. Taking a deep breath, he put one foot in front of the other walking as straight as he could to the station, the station he once thought of as his. Ted walked beside him, half-questioning and half-wondering why everyone was talking about Aaron's limited physical ability. What he didn't know was that with every step pain radiated from Aaron's spine and exploded in his head. At the entrance, Aaron stopped for a moment in an attempt to stand tall. Clenching his jaw, and using every bit of strength available, he walked up to the front desk with a smile.

A ranger, whose name Aaron could not remember, greeted him.

"Hi, Aaron, how are you? Boy you look great!"

Aaron offered a handshake, almost losing his balance. "I'm good and can't wait to get back to work."

Ted walked around the desk and signaled for the other ranger to follow him into the back room. While they were gone Aaron looked around. Some things had changed. The computer now had a flat screen, and the brochures lined up on the far table were different. It looked like the walls had been painted. The board that held the truck keys was just inside the backroom door; exactly where it had been the day Aaron took his truck up the mountain. Truck number 4433 flashed in his memory.

The men returned and asked Aaron if he would join them for lunch. Everyone agreed that Chinese take-out was the way to go. They could catch up while chowing down. Ted, grabbing the truck fob off the board, headed out to pick up their order. Meanwhile, Aaron got comfortable.

Weak from standing on his feet for so long and pain radiating up his spine, Aaron knew he needed to take his pain meds. His breathing was becoming rapid, his mouth was dry, and his head was pounding. Still forcing a smile, Aaron settled back in a chair that had wheels and allowed him to move about with ease. Andy, another Ranger, gave Aaron the latest bulletin from Forest Service Headquarters. He then went to help visitors that just arrived and had questions about a local campground and needed directions.

Aaron choked down four pain pills and attempted to read the bulletin. His vision was blurry, and it was impossible for him to see the print clearly. Anger overtook him. Balling the bulletin in his fist and throwing it on the floor, he rolled the chair over to the wall where the truck fobs were hung. He found the one for his truck - truck number 4433. Struggling to stand he lost his balance knocking the chair over with a bang. Andy glanced his way. When Aaron gave him the thumbs up and a quick forced smile, he returned his attention to the tourists. Calling on all his strength Aaron grabbed the fob off of the board and headed toward the back of the building where he knew the trucks were parked.

The parking area looked just as he remembered. All the trucks were newer, updated models and, except for two vacant spaces, all the trucks were there. The parameter of each parking space was designated with white painted borders. Each truck was parked in the space marked with its number painted in large, yellow figures.

Aaron's pain was returning and his left leg was beginning to drag. He was feeling defeated. Popping two more pain pills he reached down and dragged his leg forward. Pain shot from his spine to his heel. Another painful step forward and the bright, yellow numbers 4433 caught his eye - his truck number. With every ounce of strength he had left, he pressed the fob, opened the door, and climbed in.

Aaron could see it was a different model than his old truck and had more bells and whistles, but the ignition light went on and it started easily. As he shifted into drive and moved toward the main road, he felt like he was home.

The road looked familiar. Although his equilibrium was off from the meds kicking in, his pain level had lessened.

"Yes, this is the road I was on," he said out loud. "I remember now."

It was the first time he had any memory of the day of the accident. Others had given him an account but, until now, his memory was blank. The dirt road narrowed as the truck climbed the mountain. Ted was calling out to him over the two-way radio, but Aaron didn't respond, ignoring the relay. It was important to him to remember everything. He was sure remembering exactly what happened would help him heal. The road continued to climb as he maneuvered the familiar twists and turns. As the truck moved around the next curving stretch, standing in the middle of the winding road was a small, golden coyote.

*     *     *     *     *

Anna sat on the porch watching the sunset. Sky was in her room playing with a school friend, and Cayenne and Blackie were in the bedroom keeping watch over the girls. It had been a while since the little coyote had appeared to Anna, but there he was sitting in the setting sun, golden fur moving slowly back and forth in the breeze. He could have been a statue. Then, as if hearing something, he turned his head and ran up the driveway. Anna watched as he scurried by and disappeared into the shadows.

A cloud of dust announced Aaron's return home. But to Anna's surprise, when the truck stopped, it was Ted and Bob who got out. She waived as they approached.

"Where's Aaron?" she asked.

Ted stopped at the bottom of the stairs. Anna knew from the look on his face something was wrong.

Her voice quivered. "Where's Aaron?"

Ted's voice was soft and clear. "I'm sorry, Anna, Aaron took a truck from the Ranger Station and drove it up the mountain. He missed the turn and careened off the road and down the ravine. We'll take you to the hospital."

Anna shook her head in disbelief. "He took a truck? How did that happen? He can just barely walk!"

Ted held out his hand. "We need to take you right away. We'll tell you everything on route."

Anna recognized the urgency in Ted's voice, urgency she knew only too well.

First, she needed to call Bill. Even though it had been months since she talked to him, it was what she knew she had to do.

Anna's voice cracked as she spoke. "Bill, Aaron has had another accident. Sky is in her room with a friend. Can you help me?"

Bill heard the report over the two-way and was already headed to her house. He was on the way and would pick the girls up and take her friend home. He and Sky would meet her at the hospital as soon as he dropped her friend off.

When Anna, Ted, and Bob arrived at the emergency room Anna immediately went to admitting to get any information they had on Aaron.

The nurse entered his name into the computer and made a phone call. "Come with me, please, Mrs. Rogers."

Anna followed her through the big, double doors into a little room furnished with only a small couch and two overstuffed chairs. After a few minutes a doctor, who she had not met before, entered the room and introduced himself.

He paused for a moment before he spoke. "I'm sorry, Mrs. Rogers, your husband was pronounced dead at the scene of the accident."

Anna felt weak. The nurse held her arm and led her to a chair.

"What happened?" she asked, staring into space, avoiding the faces of those in the room.

"The report is not complete as yet but, from all indications, your husband drove up the mountain road at a high rate of speed and was unable to maneuver a sharp curve."

The doctor had no other information.

Anna, repeating to herself what she just heard, remembered that it was the same road, and the same bend as his first accident. What they were telling her today was this time the truck went down the ledge and burst into flames, ending Aaron's life. As Anna looked up, the calendar on the wall caught her attention. She recognized that it was eight years ago, exactly, that Aaron had his first accident. It was eight years ago that she made her first trip to the hospital with Bill and Ted. It was eight long years ago, and now it was finally over.

Anna's emotions rose and fell. At first, she couldn't cry, and then she couldn't stop crying. This was her worst nightmare. She was angry, sad, confused. Then she felt guilt - guilt because she was feeling relief. A wave of sadness welled inside her. Anna had no control over the flood of tears that followed. Every inch of her body ached and, when she thought her tears were done, they came flooding back again and again.

Bill and Sky arrived at the hospital and were taken immediately to Anna.

Sky ran to her mother, hugging her around the neck. "Mommy, what's the matter? Are you sick?"

Anna looked at her daughter trying to catch her breath so she could speak. "Daddy is gone. He was in an accident in his truck, and now he has gone to heaven."

Sky looked at Bill. "My Daddy is in heaven?"

Bill had been updated on latest details of the accident by the ranger who was leading the investigation. It was apparent from all indications that Aaron never hit his brakes. Bill walked over to Anna and Sky and wrapped his arms around them, holding them silently.

After a few minutes Anna stood and took Sky's hand. "Let's go home."

Bill reached out, taking Sky's other hand, and they walked silently together to the car.

*    *    *    *    *

At home Sky curled up on the couch and quickly fell asleep. Anna asked Bill if he would stay and have a glass of wine with her. He glanced at the clock, hesitated, and then agreed.

"Am I keeping you from something - someone, Bill?" Anna asked.

Bill shook his head. "No, I was thinking that maybe you want to be alone. You might need to lie down."

Anna was not ready to be alone. "I would like some company unless you have to leave." She placed two wine glasses and a bottle of Merlot on the table.

Bill sat on the chair by the kitchen counter and poured the wine.

He raised his glass. "Here's to Aaron, finally at peace."

Anna raised her glass and looked up at Bill. None of it felt real for her. At any moment, she expected to awaken from a nightmare. How she wished it was all just a bad dream. She knew she looked awful; face puffy, eyes red, and voice scratchy. Wanting to talk about something other than the accident and Aaron, she asked Bill about his job.

He smiled and took a sip of wine. "I've been working a lot. You know I took over Aaron's Forest Supervisor job. It keeps me pretty busy. I don't see Terri much since she moved, but she is well and seems to be happy. I told her about Aaron. I'm sure you'll be hearing from her soon."

Anna was not sure what she was feeling as she looked into Bill's eyes. She was torn - torn between what she wanted and needed, and what she had lost. "Sky and I have missed you. Aaron was trying to make things the way they were before the accident, but he wasn't the same. We weren't the same. I wish I could have helped him more, but -"

She stopped, her throat was closing and tears were filling her eyes. Talking about Aaron was bringing her grief to the surface once again.

Bill interrupted. "I think I should go. I'll carry Sky up to bed, and you can finish your wine. Try to get some sleep."

Anna agreed and watched Bill as he lifted a sleeping Sky and carried her up the stairs to her bedroom. Before he left, Bill told Anna he would check in on them the following day. He knew she needed to make decisions about the wake and funeral, and he would be there to help her with whatever she needed. Anna walked him to the door, closing her eyes as he left.

Cayenne and Blackie squeezed by her into the house. She had forgotten that they were still outside. Lying on the couch she pulled the comforter up to her chin and put her hand out searching for Cayenne. He moved closer, leaning in against the couch. Anna rested her hand on his back and drifted off to sleep.

*    *    *    *    *

Sky was up early the next morning asking a lot of questions. Anna answered each one carefully and simply. The message to Sky was that Daddy was in heaven. They had lots to do over the next couple of days for his goodbye service, and she needed to be helpful. Sky was happy that Uncle Bill brought them home from the hospital and asked if he would be back.

"Yes," Anna assured her, "Uncle Bill and Aunt Terri will be here for Daddy's goodbye."

She explained to Sky what the wake and funeral meant and what would be happening.

Sky sat quietly for several minutes and thought about all that her mother had said. "Does Daddy hurt anymore?"

Anna smiled. "No, Daddy doesn't hurt anymore."

Sky turned toward the door to leave. "Good. I'm going to ask my friend, Deb, to come to Daddy's goodbye."

Then she and the boys ran outside to play.

The first floor of the house was filled with Aaron's things. It was where he had lived for the past year - his last year. Anna was not yet ready to move anything, but people were coming, and she had to make some decisions.

Walking into the barn she looked around at his tools. His workshop brought back a flood of memories. The smell of sawdust and freshly cut wood reminded her of him. When he returned to the house from his workshop the fragrances of lemon and mineral oil followed him. She imagined Aaron sitting at his workbench creating a treasure from wood. She was amazed at the beautiful pieces of art he carved from what looked to her like dead limbs of trees.

It was here that he was happy and seemed pain free. Anna wondered if somehow he gave up his pain to the wood. From the vantage point of the workshop she could see his beloved mountains. Looking through the collection of wood pieces that were laying on his workbench she found a small, rectangular, wooden box. Turning it, she could see it had rough, naturally curved edges. It was beautiful. Aaron handcrafted it creating a blend of dark and light woods, forming a stunning design. He must have hand polished it to produce the smooth, elegant finish. Lifting the top of the little box she found a note tucked inside. She recognized it as Aaron's handwriting.

As she read it out loud her memory returned to their early days and reminded her of all she had lost.

It said, "For my beautiful Sky. This treasure box was made for you with all the love I have in my heart. Every grain, every curve, every nuance was fashioned with my love for you in mind. Just as the merging of these woods creates an extraordinary blend of strength and softness, life will ask you for the same. As you grow, at times you will be called on to stand strong and fight hard for what you believe in. Love requires that you hold softness in your heart, too. There is a beauty in the mix. When real love enters your life, you will recognize the blending. The mix will be familiar, a perfect fit. Never let it go. Love you forever, Daddy."

Anna held the note to her heart. Sky never really knew Aaron. She never felt his love. The truth was they had lost him a very long time ago, before she was born. Reading the note Anna knew that somewhere deep inside, passed the pain and confusion, Aaron loved them. He loved them with all his heart.

*    *    *    *    *

The wake was an endless parade of friends and coworkers. Some visitors didn't know Aaron, only knew of him, but felt moved to pay their respects. Anna, smiled, shook their hand or hugged them, and said, "Thank you," over and over again. She moved through the next couple of days automatically; no tears, smiling when appropriate, but feeling numb. She was tired, but couldn't sleep, and hungry, but couldn't eat. Terri and Bill helped out, getting her and Sky where they were supposed to be. Sky followed Bill's lead; whatever he asked her to do she did immediately. Terri helped Anna choose what to wear and placed food in front of her hoping she would eat.

*    *    *    *    *

It was all finally over. The day after the funeral was quiet. The sun beamed rays of light that looked to Anna like rods of diamond dust. Sitting on the front porch with a cup of coffee she watched the boys and Sky as they played, wondering if she would ever feel happy again. In two days, Sky would be going back to school, and she was going into the office. Anna needed structure back in her life. She hoped that getting back to her work routine would help her feel normal.

Returning to work felt right. Working her way through the day helped Anna focus on something other than the past several days – the past several years. It was good to be back in the office. She lost herself in the writing and proofreading of articles. The assignments she chose for herself allowed her to get home in time to meet Sky as she got off the school bus.

The first week back to work went well. Anna's sadness came in waves, sending her to the ladies' room for a private cry. When Friday finally came she was looking forward to the end of the day. The school bus pulled up, the door squeaked open, and Sky jumped off. Running and jumping up into Anna's outstretched arms, almost ended in a fall. Laughing at their spectacle, they walked down the driveway together with the boys following close at their heels. Anna couldn't help but feel better as she watched Sky. Running ahead with the boys following her, she hopped, skipped and jumped with youthful abandon all the way to the front door. It seemed that Sky was unaffected by the loss of her father. Cayenne and Blackie ran and jumped following Sky's lead. Anna enjoyed seeing them play. As they got closer Terri stepped from the porch to greet them.

Surprised, Anna asked, "What are you doing in these parts?"

"Just thought I'd stop by and see how everything was going. "Chinese food for supper?" Terri asked, holding up a shopping bag filled to the brim.

As she hugged Sky, Terri winked at Anna. "I'm on vacation, and thought I would visit my favorite gals."

Cayenne and Blackie got a hug and a treat from Terri, too.

It was a little early for supper, but it gave them time to catch up. During the wake and funeral, they had little time to talk.

Terri was enjoying her job at the magazine and had a new love interest. It was a man. She wasn't sure he was the one, but she liked him and was having a good time. Bill was dating someone, but said he was going to end it. When Terri asked him why, he simply said it wasn't a good fit for him. Anna felt a pang in the pit of her stomach when she heard about Bill's dating. She knew he had to live his life, but didn't want to imagine him with his arms around another woman. It was surprising to her, but she was feeling a little jealous.

Anna showed Terri the beautiful treasure box that Aaron made for Sky.

Terri read the letter aloud. When she finished, she placed it back inside. "It's beautiful. This sounds like Aaron - how I remember him before the accident."

Anna wasn't sure it was the right time to give the letter to Sky. After talking about it, they agreed it would be better to save it for when she was older. The letter would wait, but for how long Anna wasn't sure.

Terri and Anna talked about the happy times together when they were young, remembering when Aaron was funny and full of life. Anna mentioned that Aaron's totem animal showed itself to her a short time before she learned of Aaron's death.

She also thought it a strange coincidence that the nurse who called her from the hospital to tell her about the accident was Mrs. Kyotee. Terri held Anna's hand and listened without response.

Quickly changing the subject Anna asked Terri if she wanted to stay the night. Terri borrowed a pair of Anna's pajamas and slipped her feet into a pair of white athletic socks. They made popcorn and cuddled on the couch under the comforter. Their entertainment for the evening was Sky's favorite movie, "The Adventures of Baily: The Lost Puppy."

The following morning, as usual, Sky waited for the school bus, with the boys by her side, until she climbed aboard and was on her way. Then Cayenne and Blackie meandered back home and stretched out on the front porch to laze in the sun. Anna and Terri had coffee, talked about their plans for the day, and went their separate way.

*      *      *      *      *

At work Anna fought back tears throughout the day, wondering when they would stop. They came at unexpected times as sadness rose from her core and spilled out. Those she worked with pretended not to notice, but were very aware that she was struggling with a heavy heart.

It was the end of another long day. Anna and Sky celebrated the coming weekend with a treat of milk and cookies after dinner. Just as they sat trying to decide which cookies would be best, a tap on the front door drew their attention from the big cookie decision.

"Hi, Uncle Bill," Sky said, smiling. "Come and have cookies with us."

Bill smiled and stepped in to join them. "Sky, how did you know I love cookies?"

Anna was surprised to see him, but pleased he stopped by.

He explained, "I left work early to see how you two were doing today."

"Why don't you join us for dinner then?" Anna suggested.

Bill replied without hesitation. "Okay, that sounds good."

He took his jacket off and placed it across the back of a kitchen chair. Bill looked strong and handsome in his uniform. He was tall and muscular. His shaved head was new, but Anna was getting used to it. Bill's eyes were dark, and the dimple in his chin deepened when he smiled. She caught herself admiring his strong appearance and handsome face. She was even enjoying the way he smelled.

Slightly embarrassed, she cleared her throat to speak. "I don't have much in the way of groceries, but I do have some leftover Chinese food, complements of Terri. How does that sound?"

"Sounds good," Bill said, smiling at Sky who was hanging upside-down, her legs wrapped around his waist.

Lifting her up so they would be face to face, he kissed her forehead and suggested that they help Mommy set the table for supper. When the Chinese food was finished and the dishes cleared, Sky and Bill went out into the back yard. Bill watched her as she rode her bike in circles around the patio. It was beginning to get dark early, and the fall weather was cool and crisp, but Sky took the opportunity to show Uncle Bill her excellent bike riding skills.

Anna went to the back door and called them in. It was time for Sky to have a bath and get ready for bed. Bill said goodnight, kissing them both on the forehead. Before he left they casually made plans for dinner another night the following week.

Sky finished her bath, brushed her teeth, put her pink pajamas on, and climbed into bed. Her favorite bedtime storybook was sitting on her pillow waiting for Anna. She asked Uncle Bill to read to her before he left, but he said he had to go home, but promised he would read a story next time. Anna entered Sky's bedroom holding the little treasure box in her hand.

"What is that, Mommy?" Sky asked, scrunching up her face.

Opening the little wooden box Anna handed it to Sky. She had removed the letter from Aaron, deciding it would be for another time.

Anna explained, "This was made for you by Daddy with all his love."

Anna's voice got heavy. She quickly wiped the tears from her cheeks, hoping Sky did not see them. "Your Daddy was in a lot of pain from his accident. I know he seemed mad sometimes, but he loved you very much.

Sky looked into Anna eyes. "Did he love you, too, Mommy?

Hugging Sky, Anna assured her, "Yes, he loved us both."

Anna searched her memory for the last time she felt loved by Aaron. It was a long time ago, and so much had happened. She knew he loved her – them - when he told her what to name Sky from his coma. She felt love from him when he protected her, warning her to get out of the mud room before the lightning struck and, again, when he told her to go to Sky in the pond. Those were the times she knew he loved them. When he woke from the coma, she never felt that love again. He was angry most of the time, struggling with pain, medication, depression, and lack of sleep. She never again got a glimpse of the Aaron she had fallen in love with.

Anna tried to remember the last time they said I love you to each other or the last time they made love. Thinking back, she remembered the morning he left for work on the day of his first accident. She replayed the day in her mind trying to remember every detail. Anna could only smile when she thought about the morning shower they shared.

She recalled when he left that morning he placed his coffee cup on the counter and threw her a kiss, saying, "I love you, Babe."

That was it. That was the last time. It felt like a lifetime ago. Anna was a different person when Aaron awoke from his coma. She was seven years older, a mother, and a professional woman. She couldn't remember his arms around her or the feel of his lips on hers. The memory of those moments drifted away over the years he was gone. Again, her tears were uncontrollable as she grieved the loss of the love she once had, the life they once shared, and the future that was gone forever.

Sky, trying to make her mother feel better, hugged her. "Daddy is in heaven now. He isn't mad anymore; is he, Mommy?"

Anna smiled through her tears. "You're right. Let's put this little box right beside your bed. You can put all your treasures in it, so Daddy can watch over them from heaven."

Sky liked the idea that her Daddy was watching from heaven. She took her little, silver bracelets off and placed them inside the wooden box.

"There, Mommy," Sky said pointing to her end table. "There's a good place to put it. I put the bracelets that Uncle Bill gave me inside. Daddy can watch over them."

Anna shook her head in approval. She smiled, gave Sky a hug, snuggled down on the bed, and opened the storybook.

\*       \*       \*       \*       \*

Uncle Bill Night rolled around. Sky was excited and talking incessantly. Anna was busy fixing Bill's favorite dish, lasagna. Uncle Bill Night became a weekly ritual over the months since Aaron's death. The holidays were approaching, and Bill was going to take them Christmas tree shopping the following weekend. Anna felt a little guilty that life felt so good. It was months before her crying stopped, but it did, and she could finally eat. For the first time in a very long time she felt happy, and she and Bill were friends again. He brought joy back into their lives.

Bill arrived at his usual time bringing flowers: a small bouquet of yellow, tea roses for Sky and a larger bouquet of red roses for Anna. Anna was surprised and pleased by the gesture. Dinner was a hit; both Bill and Sky went in for a second helping. Dessert was cupcakes that Sky made all by herself. They were chocolate with vanilla frosting and topped with faces made of jellybean eyes and a big, red liquorish smile. Bill was very impressed with Sky's art, and she was proud of Uncle Bill's approval. After helping put the dishes in the sink, Sky skipped up the stairs to her room, followed closely by the boys. Bill helped Anna clear the table and load the remaining serving dishes into the dishwasher.

Anna was the first to speak. "Thank you for the flowers, Bill. Sky is so lucky to have you in her life."

Bill stopped what he was doing and took Anna's hands in his. "What about you, Anna? How do you feel about having me in your life again?"

Anna looked into Bill's eyes. She knew this moment would come - had hoped this moment would come. Bill stepped closer, slowly pulling her against him. She closed her eyes and leaned into his body. He kissed her lips, softly at first, then passionately. Anna's body was awakened by his lips, his strength, and his musky fragrance. She surrendered to Bill's embrace, floating at last in renewed passion.

Sky, hopping down the stairs, ended the moment with a start. They moved quickly apart, heading to opposite sides of the kitchen, as if retreating to their own corner.

Sky stopped quickly at the entrance to the kitchen. "Uncle Bill, I want to show you the little box Daddy made for me."

She handed the box to Bill with a big, proud smile. He carefully opened it to find the bracelets he had given her inside.

"Mommy said that Daddy would watch over everything I put inside the box. I want Daddy to watch over my bracelets."

Bill nodded in approval. "That's a good idea, Sky. I think your Daddy made you a beautiful jewelry box. I'm sure it was made with love."

Sky was smiling as her eyes glanced back and forth between Bill and her mother. "Uncle Bill, are you going to kiss Mommy again? I think you should kiss Mommy again."

Anna, feeling a little uneasy, cleared her throat and told Sky that it was time for Uncle Bill to go home, and she needed to get ready for bed.

Uncle Bill Nights turned into days and outings. The love that had been quiet for so long bloomed and encircled them, creating a new family.

Bill and Anna married the following year. It was a small celebration; Terri was her matron of honor, Ted was Bill's best man, and Sky was the flower girl. When rings were exchanged, Sky was included. Her forever ring was designed with a little golden heart on the band; a tiny diamond twinkled from the center. It was engraved with the wedding date and the word "*Forever.*" Bill became her father, and the three of them went to Disneyland for their honeymoon.

*    *    *    *    *

Life was good. New boys were added as the years passed, taking the place of the boys who went to the rainbow bridge; a collie named Bruce, a chocolate lab named Brownie, and a poodle named Curley. Anna left the newspaper and concentrated on writing articles for magazines and assorted blogs. Their family was strong and loving. Sky excelled academically as well as in sports. She was a natural in the kitchen and was awarded a full scholarship to Johnson and Wales, graduating with honors from the Culinary Arts Program in Rhode Island.

At Sky's graduation party, Anna noticed a young man being very attentive to her, almost always by her side. Anna thought she knew all of Sky's friends, but this man was new. She brought Bill's attention to what she was noticing. After watching them for a short time Bill agreed something was up.

"Who is the young man who is getting so much of your attention? Are you going to introduce him to us?" Anna asked Sky when they were alone.

Anna was surprised by her response. "His name is Eric. We met this year at school. He's a wonderful chef. Actually, Mom, he's been offered a job in Rome, and he's asked me to go with him. I've been meaning to talk to you and Dad about it, but I thought it would be better if I waited until after graduation."

Anna was not prepared to hear that her daughter was thinking about moving to Rome with a man they didn't know. "Are you considering it? Are you going to marry him?"

Without hesitation Sky said, "Yes, I'm considering Rome. We haven't talked about marriage. I don't think I'm ready for that, but I would love to go to Rome with him. I think I can get a job there that will be good for my career, too. What do you think, Mom?"

Anna was stunned. After some thought she said, "I have something to give you from your father- Aaron. I think now is the right time. We can talk more after your party."

Sky shrugged her shoulders and moved across the room to connect with Eric who was watching her closely. With a coy smile, she slipped her hand into his and bumped him with her hip.

Anna and Bill cleaned up while Sky walked the last of her guests to the door to say goodnight. They noticed a lingering kiss between Sky and Eric. It was evident Sky was making a statement. Anna knew immediately her daughter had already made up her mind.

When everyone was gone and the house was again quiet, Anna and Bill asked Sky to sit with them.

Anna began. "Sky, I know you're tired, but I have something for you. It's been an exciting and very long day, but this is important."

The three of them sat at the dining room table. Sky reached out and took Anna and Bill's hands in hers.

"I want to thank you so much for this wonderful party. Thank you for always being there when I needed you. I love you both so much." Then Sky lifted her brows and asked, "So, what's up?"

Anna reached into her pocket. She slowly unfolded the letter that was written long ago by Aaron. It was the letter she had been saving, waiting for just the right moment.

Handing it to Sky she said, "This is a note that your father – Aaron - wrote to you. He made the treasure box with all his love and this letter was written from his heart. It was tucked inside when I found it. I think it was the only way he knew how to show you – how to tell you how much he loved you. I saved it because I thought you were too young to understand what he was saying. I think it's time you read his final words to you."

Sky, reading the massage out loud, stopped from time to time to clear her throat and wipe away her tears. "I really didn't think that he loved me. I was afraid of him. He seemed so hard but, I guess, mixed in with all that anger, he loved me. He did love us, didn't he? Thank you for giving this to me. I'll always treasure it. I wish I could thank him."

Bill knew it was time for Sky to have Aaron's note, and he hoped it would resolve some of the questions she had about her father. Even though Aaron was her biological father, Bill had always loved Sky as if she were his own. He stood, leaned over, and kissed her forehead.

She smiled the little girl smile he knew only too well. "I love you, too. You are really the only father I've ever known."

Anna could wait no longer. "Sky, are you actually thinking about going to Rome with a young man you hardly know? This letter from your father is telling you that love is the fabric that holds lives together. Do you love this boy?"

Bill sat back down. He wanted to know more about Eric, too. "How did you meet? What do you know about him? Why have we not heard about him before now?"

Sky's shoulders visibly tightened. "Wow, I didn't expect this. As I told Mom, we met in school. He is a very talented chef and has been offered a great opportunity in Rome. I love him, and I want to go with him. My plan is to find a job in my specialty there. I haven't found one yet, but we've got contacts living in Rome from school, and they're going to help me. I'm very excited. I didn't tell you, because I wasn't sure. I've thought about it, and now I'm sure. With so much going on with the graduation and the party, I just wasn't ready to talk about it. Please be happy for me."

Anna's tone was serious. "It sounds like you've made up your mind. I guess there's nothing more to say. I don't like you going off with a boy you don't really know. I'm wondering if Rome isn't what really has you excited."

Sky tensed. "I love him. I'm going to do this whether you approve or not. I love you both, but I'm twenty-two and this is my life. I have to live it my way."

Sky turned and headed to her bedroom closing the door softly behind her.

Anna and Bill were silent for a moment.

Bill was the first to speak. "I think she is right. This is her life. Up until now she has asked our advice and made good choices. I think we have to trust her. What are you thinking?"

Anna rubbed her temples. "I know you're right, but she is still my little girl. It's so had to think of her going off to Rome. I missed her when she went away to college. I don't know when we'll see her again; she'll be so far away."

Bill smiled. "Is this about her choices or is it about you missing your daughter? I think it will give us a good excuse to take a trip to Rome next year."

Sky peeked around the corner into the kitchen. "I'm sorry. I didn't mean for this to happen this way. Eric and I were going to tell you together. He really is a good guy. Can't we have dinner together and talk a little more? When you get to know him, I'm sure you'll love him, too."

Anna and Bill agreed that it would be best if they were all there for the Rome discussion. A dinner was planned for the following night.

*     *     *     *     *

Sky was nervous and paced outside on the porch waiting for Eric to arrive. It was spring, and the front yard was bright with a green haze that floated over the ground as the new grass stretched toward the sun. Sky's attention was drawn toward the road. A little, golden coyote darted back and forth as if calling her to play, and then he was gone.

Although he was late, Eric arrived with a bouquet of roses for Anna and a box of cigars for Bill. Bill wasn't a smoker, but accepted the gift gratefully, thinking how much Ted would enjoy them. After dinner, Sky and Anna cleared the table while Bill and Eric went into the living room to sit down.

Bill, who had been mostly quiet during dinner, began the conversation. "Eric, this job you have in Rome, is it a good paying job? I mean, will you be able to support the two of you? After all, Sky doesn't have a job right now. It will take some time for her to find one. Are you sure you will be able to make it work financially?"

Eric was prepared for the question. "I will be in training for three months. After that, I will take over as master chef and an income that is comparable in the industry. So, we'll have to be careful in the beginning but, once I'm at full pay, we'll be in good shape. As you know, Sky is a very talented pastry chef, and I believe it won't take her long to find a job. My plan is to work in Rome for five years and return to the U.S. to open my own restaurant. That's the plan anyway. I don't want you to worry about Sky; I'll take good care of her."

Sky and Anna joined the men in the living room. Sky took Eric's hand. "Okay, Dad, what have you guys been talking about?"

Bill smiled and looked at Anna. "It sounds like they have a plan. I think you'll agree they have thought this through."

Anna took Bill's lead. They were young, but what a wonderful time of life to share in Rome.

How could she possibly stop them? "If this is what you really want, it's what you should do."

Sky hugged Anna and Bill. Then she and Eric walked outside and talked under the full moon lit sky. After several good night kisses, he was on his way. As she waved goodbye, Sky again noticed the golden coyote sitting at the end of the drive-way. When she went back inside, she mentioned that she had seen the coyote twice that day. Anna agreed it was unusual. Coyotes had made appearances over the years, but not usually more than a few times a year and never twice in one day.

Anna laughed. "You know the coyote was your father's totem animal. I saw them more often when your father was alive. I haven't seen one very often since he passed away. Maybe he showed up to check Eric out."

Anna told Sky about the Vision Quest her father had taken when he was fif-teen. Aaron was proud of his time in the forest when he braved the elements to in-vite his totem animal to appear. It was a great story. Anna enjoyed telling Sky about the adventure as much as Sky enjoyed hearing it. It was a happy memory of Aaron they could share.

Sky was on cloud nine. She and Eric planned to travel to Europe and make a life together. His job as chef of Casa Maesto in Rome was exciting to think about. The restaurant specialized in contemporary Italian cuisine and was a perfect train-ing ground for his future plans. They were taking the first step in the direction of Eric's dream.

Everything was in place. Sky convinced her mother and Bill that it was what she wanted and, as soon as she got settled, she would pursue her dream of becom-ing a pastry chef. Their approval came with a three-month allowance to get them through Eric's training period. That gave them a little breathing room financially and would buy some time, so Sky could find a job that she really wanted.

Bill and Anna never had the opportunity to spend much time with Eric before they left; it seemed he was always busy. Sky assured them again and again that he was an honest, hardworking man, who made her happy.

Sky and Eric purchased their tickets, and Sky searched the internet to find a place in Rome for them to live. Only two weeks before their departure date, she found what looked to her to be the perfect place. It was a furnished one room apart-ment close to where Eric would be working. The site listed all the statistics and offered photos. Sky was impressed with the beautiful living space. From the first time she saw the pictures, she could imagine Eric and her living there. Of all the flats she looked at online, this one was the closest to having everything she wanted. Best of all, it was at a price they could afford.

The apartment, fully furnished, had an open floor plan with a small efficiency kitchen. The dining area offered a classic, mahogany dining room table and six matching chairs. The chairs were accented with cushions finished in a white, brocade material. It was a small space, but beautiful. Both of the white, brocade living room couches opened to a double bed and served as the sleeping space. The walls were painted white, except for the red, brick wall of the efficiency kitchen. Sky thought the space reflected a combination of light and warmth, just what she was looking for. Eric agreed and gave her the go-ahead to lease it. Sky excitedly showed her mother their soon-to-be home. Anna, too, thought it was beautiful and gave her approval, making Sky's day complete.

Unimportant to Eric but bringing Sky delight was, in addition to the living space, the back doorway from the kitchen opened to stairs carved of stone. Curving upward, the stairway ended at the entrance to a private garden. There, a marbled, glass and white, wrought iron table, and four strikingly ornate chairs, invited dining. Vine covered, mauve stucco walls kept the space private. It was markedly different from her garden at home, but there was a garden and that made her happy.

Sky visited her soon to be home online almost every day. She looked forward to having the outdoor retreat and imagined Eric and her having a glass of wine as they toasted their life together sitting outside under the stars. The photos were colorful and offered a panoramic view of the garden. It showed brightly colored flowers flourishing in earthen pots. Each pot, a different height and size, sat in repeating clusters along the wall and corners of the cobblestone patio. Above, draping vines created a canopy that dipped and flowed, partnering with the breeze. Sky thought of it as her little piece of heaven and couldn't wait for their first dinner there.

*　　*　　*　　*　　*

Sky and Eric packed lightly for their move, planning to buy anything else they would need. The plan was to get settled in, and then learn to navigate the area. Some of their American contacts lived nearby, and a get-together was on the list of things to do the first week after their arrival. The second week Eric was scheduled to start at Casa Maesto and take the first step in his career. He was a little nervous, but looking forward to the challenge. Somehow, he managed to make his job the topic of most of their conversations whether alone or with friends. Sky understood, she was certain the time would come when she, too, would have an exciting new job to talk about.

Sky was confident she would find a job in her field, and was grateful that her mother and Bill supported her success, both emotionally and financially. She was certain the three months allowance would give them time to get on their feet. Sky was very good with money and planned on working with Eric to keep his spending in line. Their financial situation was a subject Eric was not at ease talking about. In spite of what he told Bill, he was more of a "fly by the seat of your pants" kind of guy, but Sky felt she could handle their bottom line easily.

*     *     *     *     *

The goodbyes at the airport were tear-filled. Sky and Eric were hopeful and excited about the future. Sky hugged Anna and Bill, hanging on a little longer and hugging a little tighter before she let go.

Eric's sister came to the airport unexpectedly to wish her brother well. It was the first time Sky met anyone from his family. There was a strong resemblance, but there was no time for them to get to know each other. The only thing Sky really knew about Eric's family was that his mother and father had a lot of money, and Eric and his sister were expected to make their own way in life. Eric didn't speak of them often, but when he did, Sky thought they sounded distant and judgmental.

The day he excitedly told his parents about his job offer in Rome, their response was, "Will you be waiting on tables or working in the kitchen?"

To Sky, the words would have been hurtful, but Eric was unaffected.

Moving through airport security took considerable time. Sky and Eric worried that they'd miss their flight but, luckily, they arrived at the gate just in time to board. It was a long flight, approximately nine and half hours. In addition, Rome time was six hours behind East Coast time. They knew they'd have to adjust to their new surroundings, but the time change was their first big adjustment. Even though exhausted from all they had to do before they left, neither of them could sleep on the flight. They excitedly talked about their plans for the future and the life that was no longer just a dream, but a reality.

Arriving on time, they waited patiently to deplane. It felt good to stand and move around after being confined in the passenger seat of the plane for so long. In Rome, it was a balmy sixty-five degrees. After luggage pickup, they flagged a taxi. The air was slightly misty and the lights, traffic, and Italian flags waving in the breeze, felt like a welcoming party. There was so much they wanted to see: the

Colosseum, the Pantheon, the Spanish Steps, and St. Peter's Square. This was only the beginning of their new life together. Sky inhaled the fragrance of Rome and told herself she would never forget how she was feeling at that moment.

*     *     *     *     *

The studio flat was everything they hoped it would be; eight hundred square feet of pure heaven. A celebratory bottle of champagne and a framed, family picture was waiting for them on the dining room table, compliments of Anna and Bill. The couple toasted to their past, present, and future life together. Then they opened the sofa bed and allowed their tired bodies to relax and drift off to sleep at last.

The morning sun shined brightly through the dining area sliders waking Sky. Still wearing the clothes she traveled in, she slipped out of bed and rummaged through her suitcases looking for something to change into. Eric woke, extended his hand to her and pulled her back to bed. They agreed making love was a great way to start the day.

There was no food in the apartment, so after the lovemaking, they showered, dressed, and walked up the narrow, side street to the main street. The apartment buildings all looked similar with two large, picture windows on each floor, and a wooden front door entrance. Every building was a slightly different, muted color. Some had small window boxes filled with multi colored flowers. Sky loved the pastel hues and changing rainbow of color that traveled along the cobblestone roadway. The street was abuzz with buses and motorcycles weaving in and out of traffic, honking horns, and cars suddenly coming to a screeching halt. Amazingly, they didn't witness one accident.

Eric hailed a cab. Using his best Italian, he told the driver they wanted to be taken to a local coffee house for breakfast.

The driver shook his head and said, "Yes, yes, Tazza d'Orreo, one of best, tourists and locals. I'll take you. You'll not be sorry."

On the way the driver, who spoke a combination of Italian and English, asked them where they were from and how long they were going to be in Rome. He also made several suggestions of what they should see; places off the beaten path they might want to investigate. They tipped him well. He was informative, entertaining, and he offered to come back in an hour and pick them up. Sky felt like they had made a friend.

Tazza d'Orreo was bustling with activity and offered standing room only. The cabbie told them the café was family owned, first opening in the forties. It was considered by many to have the best coffee in Rome. He recommended they try granita di caffe'con panna. Sky and Eric had no idea what they were ordering but, when they took their first sip, they agreed it was wonderful. The cabbie had not steered them wrong.

Sky and Eric knew from their research, and from conversations with their American friends in Rome, they wouldn't find the eggs and bacon breakfast they were accustomed to. Italians mostly enjoyed a croissant or yogurt with a cup of coffee or a cappuccino for their first meal of the day. Many preferred morning tea around ten or eleven, which included a sandwich with thin slices of ham and cheese.

It was now ten o'clock in the morning, and they were famished. Sandwiches and cappuccino sounded like exactly what they needed. The cabbie was right; they never would have guessed that a ham and cheese croissant would taste so good for breakfast. Their conversation was infused with excitement and curiosity. Sky was in awe of everything they had seen so far and wished she could share her experience with her mother and Bill but, due to the time difference, she would have to wait. There would be lots more to tell them by the time they spoke. It was only their first morning, and they could see they had much more to learn. Sky made a mental note that she would recreate the wonderful pastry they had just savored.

Voices speaking several different dialects surrounded them, but English was obviously spoken by the employees and many of the customers. They agreed this was at the top of their list of favorite places, and they definitely were going to focus more on learning the language.

*     *     *     *     *

Returning to the apartment they sorted through their belongings trying to decide where to put everything in the beautiful but limited space. There was only one small closet. This was the first time in their relationship they had shared space. Most of their time together was spent in one of their dorm rooms. Now, decisions had to be made that would affect them both. They took the leap from dating and sharing space in a dorm from time to time, to living in a foreign country as a couple. This was a major adjustment for them both.

A celebratory romp under the covers ensued after finding a place for the last item in the suitcase. They laughed and made fun of each other's awkward attention to favorite body parts and fell asleep wrapped in each other's arms.

*       *       *       *       *

Their first week in Rome was a whirlwind of hailing cabs, sightseeing, being lost, finding their way, meeting new people, and eating, eating, eating. They laughed, delighting in their time together, and made love over and over again.

Eric's first day of work gave Sky time to think about her future. Her next priority was to find a job. They were settled into their apartment and met with their American contacts who provided Sky with inside information on several job opportunities. She was hoping one would be a good fit for her talent and ability. Their first three months were financed by her mother and Bill, so Sky was comfortable enough to be a little choosey. She felt there was time to find just the right job. Her real desire was to have what Eric had, a job that fit her skills and offered a stepping stone to a successful culinary future. Sky knew the move to Rome was to ensure Eric's career, not hers, but she had faith in her ability and intended to find a job that fit her talent as a pastry chef. For her, it was exciting and a little frightening.

Eric's job quickly consumed his time and energy. He worked long hours and slept until noon. When he arose, he dressed silently and immediately light up a cigarette. He quit smoking at Sky's request before they left for Rome but, now, not only was he smoking again, he was smoking heavily.

Sky quietly watched him dress as she lay in bed. She thought he looked handsome in his uniform. It included a toque, the chef's hat, a white double-breasted jacket, and a houndstooth patterned black and white pair of pants. He had to be impeccably dressed every day. To ensure perfection his uniforms were provided and cleaned by the restaurant.

Eric's biggest challenge in the morning was getting out of bed. Before he left the apartment, he made himself a giant mug of black coffee to go, and then headed out on the motorcycle he purchased secondhand shortly after they arrived. They quickly discovered that a motorcycle was the cheapest and most viable means of transportation for him to take back and forth to work. Eric enjoyed his morning and evening rides to and from the restaurant. They cleared his head as he imagined all the stress of his day blowing away as he rode through the streets of Rome. It was also the most convenient transportation for almost everything they did in-between. Sky was not comfortable driving the motorcycle, but was content to be a passenger. The bus system worked best for her, and she became adept at getting wherever she needed to be with ease.

*     *     *     *     *

Eric's restaurant opened at 4:00 P.M. closing at 10:45 P.M. His workday began at one o'clock in the afternoon. His time was spent in food preparation and supervision of the kitchen staff. It was his first supervisory position, and he wanted to standout, however, the head chef's close oversight made him uncomfortable. Eric knew he had a lot to learn. Eager to please, he went above and beyond expectations, fueling his energy with caffeine and nicotine.

When the restaurant closed in the evening Eric directed the kitchen staff in cleanup and reviewed the next day's menu. His days were long and challenging. When done, he went home to a dark apartment and a sleeping Sky. Not ready for sleep himself, he sat in the dining area and read his hometown newspaper on the internet while drinking wine, until he unwound and was ready for bed.

Sky waited up for Eric to come home after work for the first several weeks, wanting to hear about his day. Sometimes she fell asleep, waking in time to join him for a glass of wine and hear about his latest frustration or triumph.

Her days were long and lonely. Although she thought she had several job options, they turned out to be mostly waitress positions. She was excited to be in Rome and happy that Eric's career was taking off, but she was unemployed, alone most of the day, and was missing home.

For the first several months Eric slept until noon on his days off. When he awoke they packed a lunch and set out to experience the magic of Rome. It was everything Sky had imagined; bubbling with history, art, amazing architecture, and simple neighborhood trattorias. And the food - The food was marvelous. Eric talked about his job incessantly, but he was puzzled why Sky hadn't found one. The three months' allowance from Anna and Bill was coming to an end. He was feeling pressured and was afraid they would be unable to support themselves without income from Sky.

The cobblestone roads and narrow side streets, filled with people walking and scooters humming, were very different from the small, New Hampshire town Sky grew up in. In Rome, the traffic on the main street was bumper-to-bumper with every description of compact car, blazing horns, and motorcycles revving. For Sky the sounds were a symphony, and she thought every excursion they took was exciting. Chronicling their outings on her phone camera, she sent the photos to her mother and Bill and shared each of their wonderful adventures.

Eric was most impressed with the history of the rise and fall of the Roman Empire; the statues and paintings. Each of the cafés they visited offered a treat for their pallet and a delightful, firsthand experience in fresh Mediterranean cuisine. Sky was learning quite a bit about the local eateries and what the visitors wanted and enjoyed. Both were getting better at understanding and speaking Italian.

Eric's one day off a week gave them their only real time together. They called it Rome day. Sky planned each free day, intending to visit places of interest that offered Roman architecture, history, art, and magnificent cuisine. Always included in their excursion were simple neighborhood trattorias and art studios. On their list of most desired sites to see were the major wonders of Rome. When the motorcycle was not practical, the subway and bus system offered them freedom to move throughout the city. Taking the motorcycle was not Sky's first choice. She sat closely behind Eric with her arms wrapped tightly around his waist, keeping her eyes closed as they traveled the busy, narrow streets of Rome.

The Trevi Fountain was on the top of Sky's list of must see. According to folk lore, if a coin was tossed into the fountain with the right hand, it ensured a return to Rome. It was the largest Baroque fountain in the City and one of the most famous in the world. For Sky, it was magical. Eric was not interested in the folklore; he was impressed with the sheer magnitude of the architecture.

\*　　\*　　\*　　\*　　\*

Eric was changing his mind. He chose not to discuss his newly adjusted career path with Sky. Confident that everything was working just as he planned, he was rethinking his projected move back to the States. He was unsure he wanted to leave Rome.

When they arrived at the four-month mark, money was getting tight. Eric was making enough to pay the bills, but there was little left for anything else. Sky was searching for a job that fit her background, but she was now ready to take anything.

Helen, one of her American friends working in Rome, gave her a heads-up. Café Roma was looking for help. It was close to their apartment, and they wanted someone who could speak English.

The interview went well. Sky's Italian was good enough to sort through orders given to her in Italian and she, of course, was perfect for their English-speaking customers. The owner was impressed with her background, but was clear he only wanted her for sandwich making, waiting on tables, taking customer's orders, and taking pizza out of the brick oven. The pay was not what she hoped for, but it was the only job offer she had in over a month. Sky took the job and reported for work at 7:00 A.M. the following morning. It was a baptism of emersion.

*     *     *     *     *

Anna worried about Sky. They spoke daily and, at first, Sky sounded happy. As the months passed, although she was saying she was happy and busy, Anna sensed she wasn't hearing the full story. Bill assured her Sky was getting settled in and reminded her that their daughter was a grown woman. He was confident she could handle whatever came along.

What Sky was not telling her mother about was her day-to-day grind. Five days a week she left a sleeping Eric at 6:30 A.M. in the morning and headed to work. He slept until noon. Sky returned home at 5:30 P.M., collapsing into their empty bed, exhausted from being on her feet all day. Eric usually arrived home around one in the morning. It became his practice to join his kitchen crew for drinks and conversation after hours. Their bills were being met, and Eric was developing as a manager and making friends. Sky, however, was waiting on tables and making sandwiches. She was feeling lonely and unfulfilled.

The time difference and work hours made the weekday phone calls home impossible; weekends were easier. Sunday was best for their "catch up" phone call that worked for both time zones. Anna and Bill looked forward to the Sunday conversations with their daughter. It made them feel more like a part of her life. Sky sometimes dreaded them, struggling to find her happy voice and good news to share.

Bill was concerned that Sky was settling. She was a graduate of Johnson and Wales, a one-hundred-year-old institution with a superlative culinary arts program. She had been a standout in her class. He found it difficult to accept that she was happy to be making sandwiches. This was not the life they imagined for their daughter. Sky's dream was to specialize in desserts and, perhaps, teach. Like Bill, Anna also believed their daughter had much more to offer the world. Although they wanted Sky to be the one to decide to make changes, they wondered how long it would take her to recognize change was needed.

*     *     *     *     *

Finally, a day off together gave them time they could share. Sky was looking forward to spending it with Eric. Her plan was to pack a lunch and ride the countryside with him. They could find a comfortable spot to eat, toast to their new life, and enjoy each other's company. It had been a while since they had free time to do whatever they wanted. She happily put the lunch basket together; a bottle of Eric's favorite wine, fruit, and fresh croissant sandwiches.

Eric dragged himself out of bed at 10:00am. He had again stayed out later than usual the night before and was moving very slowly. Sky was dressed and ready to enjoy the day. He, however, was less eager.

Getting the signal that he was disinterested in anything she had planned, Sky asked, "Eric, are you feeling okay?"

Eric looked at her rubbing his forehead. "I had too much vino after work. I think I need to go back to beer. Can we do this lunch thing another time? I need some sleep."

Sky's disappointment and rising anger were evident. "What do you mean? We planned this day together weeks ago. I miss seeing you. I want to hear about your job and your friends. I want to tell you about my job. You can sleep later."

Eric walked into the bathroom and closed the door. "I need sleep more than I need a picnic."

It was apparent the day she planned was not going to happen. Eric could not function. Sky decided that she wasn't going to spend the day watching him sleep - not again. Picking up the lunch basket, she grabbed a light jacket and slammed the door behind her. Eric crawled back into bed, pulling the covers over his head with a groan.

Sky fastened the lunch basket to the back of her bicycle. She was angry. In her mind, she could hear the music from *The Wizard of Oz*. The scene when the witch was riding the bike across the sky flashed through her mind: dun ta dun ta dun dun. This was not how she saw her life. She weaved in and out of traffic until she reached the quiet of the countryside.

The day was warm, and the sun lit up the mountains in the distance. It brought her back to her childhood in the White Mountains of New Hampshire. Finding a spot that offered a panoramic view, she set up her picnic for one.

Sky was determined not to cry. She was angry – angry that Eric did not make their time together a priority. Focusing on her picnic she spread her blanket, carefully placing a wine glass, dish, and napkin in the center. This was supposed to be their day. She wanted to tell him about her job and hear everything about his. They never had time together anymore. Sex had been missing from their relationship for weeks. In the beginning, they made time to make love. She wondered why it had changed.

Settling down, she poured herself a glass of wine and popped a grape into her mouth. Thoughts of her father weighed heavily on her mind. He had been distant and uninvolved in her life. Her mother told her how much he loved her, but she never felt that love. She wanted a relationship like the one her mother and Bill had. Sky always knew that Bill loved her, and she could feel his love. Eric was handsome and intelligent, and she thought he loved her, but now she wasn't sure. Maybe she was just having a bad day. She hoped it would all be better tomorrow. As she tipped her glass to sip some wine, a small golden coyote appeared in the middle of the emerald green, rolling field before her. It stood motionless and seemed to be focused on her. She blinked, thinking it might be a cat or a dog she was seeing. There was no mistake it was a coyote. She wondered if she should be afraid, but she wasn't. As quickly as it appeared, it was gone.

Sky thought about her father once again. She remembered the story of his Vision Quest and the coyote that visited his sacred circle. She knew the story by heart and knew, from that day forward, the little coyote became his totem animal. Now, it was showing itself to her. Was she imagining it, or could it be a message from her father? She decided to talk to her mother about it and see what she thought.

Sky finished her lunch, packed up, and headed home. Eric was not home when she arrived. He didn't leave a note, just the empty, unmade bed. Sky called her mother. After the usual how are you and miss you conversation, she brought up the coyote. Carefully she described her day, leaving out Eric's inability to join her. The big question she had for her mother was about the appearance of her father's totem animal at her picnic.

Anna was surprised to hear from Sky, it was not their usual Sunday scheduled call. She listened quietly to her daughter as she described her day, trying to determine what the call was really about.

After considering what Sky told her, Anna answered very carefully. "Sky, I'm glad you called to tell me about this. We know the coyote was your father's totem animal, and I believe it's possible that it was visiting you for a reason."

Sky persisted. "Mom, I haven't thought of Dad's totem for years. I remember the story. Do you really believe that stuff?"

Thinking back, Sky was not sure if her mother was just telling her father's story or if she believed in signs sent from the spirit world.

Anna wanted to be very clear. "I know your father believed in it. And some things have happened in my life that I cannot explain. So, yes, I believe we sometimes get messages. Do you remember telling me that your Daddy spoke to you when he was in the coma?"

Sky thought for a moment. "I'm not sure, Mom, it seems like a dream. It was so long ago."

Anna wished she could be more help. "Why don't you think about it for a while; maybe something will come back to you. We can talk again. I really do believe your Daddy is trying to tell you something."

Sky liked the idea that her father might be saying hello. Of course, it could have just been a little, golden coyote playing in the sunshine. Either way, she had to talk to Eric and tell him what was on her mind.

*    *    *    *    *

Sky waited up. It was midnight when Eric got home, and it was obvious to Sky that he had been drinking. Even though he told her he stopped smoking, the smell of cigarettes lingered in the air around him and permeated his clothes.

Standing with her arms crossed over her chest she asked, "Where have you been? Why is it you manage to go out drinking with your friends, but you can't get out of bed to have lunch with me?"

Eric walked by Sky, stopped, and looked back at her with a sheepish grin. "Let's get married. I want you to be my wife."

Sky was not expecting a proposal. She hadn't been thinking about marriage. All she wanted was some of Eric's attention. His proposal came as a complete surprise.

The only thing she could say was, "Let's talk about it tomorrow when you are thinking clearly."

Eric agreed. Stumbling slightly, he climbed into bed. In seconds he was asleep, snoring loudly. Sky poured herself a glass of wine and went out into the garden to think. The night air was cool, but comfortable. She looked up and saw a falling star moving across the sky. She wasn't sure how she was feeling about her life. Marriage had not been part of their conversation. Sky was sometimes happy, sometimes homesick. She liked the people she worked with, but she had much more skill than the job required. Maybe it was time for her to ask for more responsibility and more involvement in baking. They knew her now, and she was sure they trusted her. Sky wondered if the coyote was telling her that it was time to make some changes.

In the morning Sky left for work before Eric awoke. She wasn't sure how she felt about his proposal. It could have been a desperate attempt to dodge her anger or, maybe, it was the rambling of too much wine. If the coyote was a sign from her father, what exactly was he trying to tell her? Was he in favor of what she was doing or was he telling her to go home?

The night after speaking with her mother Sky had a vivid dream. She was somehow in danger and a voice came from nowhere saying, "Stop now!"

She needed to talk to her mother again about her dream, but today she was going to speak to her manager and ask if he was willing to give her more responsibility. That felt right to her.

*       *       *       *       *

The café was busy from the time she arrived until closing. Sky didn't get a chance to speak to her manager, Lorenzo, during the day. She was slightly apprehensive, but he had been very supportive, even taking her under his wing teaching her the basics of café management. It was unexpected, not part of the discussion when he hired her. He was also the first to lend a hand when she needed it. Sky considered him more of a friend than a boss.

Lingering after hours with a cappuccino in hand, Sky approached Lorenzo as he was getting ready to leave.

"Lorenzo, can we talk?" she said softly, nervously holding her cup close to her chin.

"Of course, Sky, what can I help you with?" he said flashing a smile.

Sky noticed he had perfect teeth. "I know you hired me mostly as a waitress, but I'm so much more capable than that. I am a graduate of Johnson and Wales

Culinary Institute, and I'm really, really good at creating pastry. I think that's where my greatest skill lays. I would like the chance to show you. I know I can create desserts that will compliment what you already offer. You're missing out on a resource by not taking advantage of my training. I'm really an excellent pastry chef."

With only a brief hesitation, Lorenzo responded. "Okay, come in tomorrow morning an hour earlier then usual, and we'll talk about what you can do for us. Maybe it's time for some fresh ideas."

Sky was surprised that he agreed so easily. "Great! I'll see you in the morning then."

The bus ride home was crowded, but Sky didn't mind. She was feeling pleased with herself and the possibility of an exciting new opportunity. Once they agreed on what she could do to enhance their pastry menu she would bring up the subject of a wage increase.

The next issue she had to deal with was Eric's marriage proposal. Sky wasn't sure if she wanted to be married, but she didn't want to lose Eric either. So much had happened so fast. She was on cloud nine thinking about how well her conversation went with Lorenzo, and she was sure it would take some of the financial pressure off their relationship.

*     *     *     *     *

Sky arrived home and made dinner, putting half on the back of the stove for Eric as she always did. Then she called her mother to tell her the exciting news. Forgetting what time it was on the East Coast, Sky noticed her mother sounded like she had been woken up.

Even though she was feeling bad about waking her, she shared her good news. "Mom, today I asked for more responsibility making desserts. Guess what? Lorenzo agreed. I'm going to help create a new pastry menu for the café! I couldn't wait to tell you and Dad. I'm so excited."

Anna was awakened by Sky's phone call, but she was happy that she called and pleasantly surprised by the good news.

Trying not to wake Bill, Anna whispered. "Well, Sky, that's wonderful. I was wondering how long you were going to wait on tables. Dad is sleeping right now, but I'll tell him the good news first thing in the morning."

Jumping to another subject Sky continued. "I had a dream the other night. I was in danger. Something was about to fall on me and a voice told me to stop.

After that, I was floating in water. It's funny; I wasn't afraid. Does any of this make sense to you?"

Anna was surprised. "When you were five, you almost drowned. I found you because, I believe, your Daddy told me where you were. He was in a coma at the time. You also told me when you were a little girl that your Daddy warned you not to climb on your bureau, because it was going to fall on you. Do you remember any of that?"

Sky was silent for a moment. "I'm not sure. I have to think about this a little more. Mom, the coyote that I saw other day, what do you think about that?"

Anna again answered cautiously. "I know we talked about your Daddy's Vision Quest and the coyote that showed up. If I remember correctly, according to American Indian folk lore, it represents a teacher that provides guidance around life's obstacles. It is also considered a trickster. Now, let me ask you, is there something in your life that is causing you to doubt yourself?"

Sky decided to tell her mother what was going on. "Eric asked me to marry him."

That was not what Anna was expecting. "Does that make you happy?"

Still not sure of what she was feeling, Sky admitted her doubt. "I don't want to make a big mistake. Do you think marrying Eric would be a mistake?"

Anna hesitated. "Sky, you are an intelligent, beautiful, young woman. I know if you trust your instincts you'll make the decision that's right for you. Do you love Eric enough to spend the rest of your life with him? If you do, I have to wonder why you're asking me this question."

Both answering her mother and thinking out loud, Sky said, "Yes, Mom, I know what you're saying is right. I have so much going on right now. I'm going to talk to Eric tonight when he gets home. I'll give you a call tomorrow."

The following morning Anna told Bill about her conversation with Sky. They then discussed a trip to Rome for a visit, but decided it would be best if Sky made this decision herself. They agreed that the best thing they could do for their daughter was to guide her, not tell her what she should do.

\*     \*     \*     \*     \*

Sky kept thinking about the coyote. She wondered if it was possible that her father was telling her that her boundaries were being tested. From the first time she met Eric, she was enchanted. Could it be he was a trickster? She had to re-evaluate everything she had done over the last several months. Sky was looking forward to her new responsibilities at the café, it felt right to her. Her biggest question was about a life with Eric. Was it what she really wanted?

When Eric got home that night Sky was waiting up for him. He smelled of wine and cigarettes as he usually did. Eric was surprised that she was still awake. He walked toward her, arms outstretched.

Slightly slurring, he said, "Well, this is a nice surprise. Usually you are asleep when I get home. To what do I owe this pleasure? Did you decide that you are going to marry me?"

Sky moved her cheek towards him as he leaned in to kiss her lips.

"I think we should talk," was all she could say.

Straightening up quickly he ran his hand through his hair. "This sounds serious. You aren't going to turn me down, are you?"

Sky had to admit that he looked cute in a crumpled sort of way, and she was very attracted to him. His light brown hair was a little longer than she liked, but his baby blue eyes had captured her attention from the first time they met in cooking lab. The chef paired them up because they had similar cooking styles. When Eric spoke to Sky, she was immediately drawn in by his amazing smile. It didn't take long before they were spending as much time together outside the cooking lab as when they were creating a new pastry to impress the chef. The first time they made love was incredible. Sky had very little experience in that department, but Eric took his time and was a gentle, considerate lover. He was everything she wanted in a man. Today he asked her to marry him, and she wondered why she was having second thoughts.

Sky had to ask, "Eric, you know that I love you, don't you?"

Eric smiled. "Of course I do. What's wrong?"

Now that they were face-to-face, she was feeling a little silly, but said what was on her mind. "I'm feeling like I'm not important to you any more. I hardly ever see you. You seem to have time for your friends after work, but not for me. I miss us."

He took her hand. "I know I haven't been present, but I've been focused on doing the best I can with this job. It's taken most of my energy. I needed to get to know the people that work for me, so I can be a better manager. I did it for us. Now, I'm feeling comfortable and would like to concentrate more on us."

Sky thought for a moment and hesitantly asked, "I was thinking maybe you wanted someone else."

Eric smiled. "Are you kidding? Sky, you are the only woman for me."

Looking into his eye she was captured and, surprising herself, she said, "Yes. Yes, Eric, I'll marry you."

The engagement was sealed with a kiss followed by a bottle of red wine, a wonderful dessert, and passionate sex. Sky couldn't remember being happier.

*    *    *    *    *

Keeping the nine-hour time difference in mind, Sky set her phone alarm for 8:00 P.M. East Coast time. Finally connecting with her mother and Bill she excitedly told them about the wedding.

They were going to keep it small. "It will be just you and Dad, and a couple of our friends. We are aiming for next month. Will you be able to make arrangements to be here sometime in May? We'll set the date when you confirm when you can be here. There isn't enough room in our apartment for all of us, so we thought we could stay at the Plazzo Navono and celebrate together there. Please, please say you'll come."

Anna didn't hesitate. "Of course we'll be there, if that's what you want. In fact, I'm going to get right on it. I know Dad will do whatever he has to do to get the time off. I'll give you a call as soon as we have the details, and we'll go from there. If you're happy, I'm happy. Sky, I love you."

Anna hung up and called Bill immediately. He was not as willing to celebrate Sky's decision, especially after the phone call just days before. Anna was happy for her but she, too, had concerns. They agreed they needed to be there for Sky. This would be a big moment in her life, and they would make arrangements to be present for their daughter's wedding in Rome. They hoped when they arrived in Rome they wouldn't see that she was really just being swept up in the emotions of her changing life and the excitement of the wedding plans.

When Eric got home from work Sky was waiting for him. She was still on a high from talking to her mother and Bill. The plans for the wedding were forming nicely, and she was satisfied with how the details were evolving. They sat down with a glass of wine and toasted to their next step.

As Eric lifted his glass he spoke softly. "You are the woman I want to be with for the rest of my life. I want to share everything with you, and I want you to be the mother of my children."

Sky was dizzy with all that was happening and loved that Eric wanted her to be the mother of his children. They had never discussed children. It felt as though her life was finally coming together. Her job was expanding to include what she loved most, and Eric was showing her how much he loved her and needed her in his life.

As she raised her glass she beamed. "I know my father is watching over us. I wish he were alive to meet you, the love of my life."

\*     \*     \*     \*     \*

The next few weeks flew by for Sky. Bill and her mother were scheduled to arrive the last week in May. Sky made all the wedding arrangements. Although she wanted her mother to help pick out her wedding gown, she knew it wasn't practical to wait until she arrived in Rome. After talking to some of her friends, she found a small bridal shop and fell in love with the perfect wedding dress. It was simple and flattered her petite frame. Finding just the right shoes took longer than anything else. The ceremony and reservations at Plazzo Navona were confirmed. Everything was in place.

Eric was not able to help with the preparations. His work days were still long, and he was rarely available for input. Sky made all the arrangements and, when Eric got home, she ran them by him. He was always in agreement with whatever she had in mind.

Excitedly, Sky told him the details of the big day. "Mom and Dad will arrive at 8:00 P.M. on Friday. They'll have a little time to adjust to the time change before our wedding day. Our ceremony will be short. I hope you have written your vows. There is a total of ten guests. After we're married, Plazzo Navona has a small, private room where we'll have our party. Mom and Dad will go home the following day. I wish they could stay longer, but Dad has to get back to work."

Eric yawned and shook his head in approval. "It all sounds good to me. I'm beat, and I have to get some sleep."

Not being put off by his lack of enthusiasm, Sky continued. "We need to talk about our honeymoon. Where would you like to go? I was thinking maybe Tuscany. How do you feel about Tuscany?"

Again, Eric nodded in agreement. "Yeah, sure, Tuscany sounds great. Good night, Sky. We can talk more in the morning."

Sky knew there would be no talk in the morning. She had to leave for work and would be long gone before Eric got out of bed.

Sky reminded herself that he was working long days and had a lot of responsibilities.

Next on her list of things to do before she left for work was laundry. The following day, after work, she would clean the apartment. Even though her mother and Bill weren't going to stay there, they would most certainly want to see where she and Eric were living. Sky had to go food shopping, too. She drifted off to sleep reviewing everything she had to do before she could relax and enjoy herself - enjoy her wedding day.

*  *  *  *  *

At work Lorenzo watched Sky as she created another new pastry for the café to offer. He was an outstanding cook in his own right. Trained by his father his focus was pizza, croissants, and specialty dishes. Lorenzo was ready to order whatever new ingredients were needed for her menu additions, but there was no need. She was able to improvise and create mouthwatering pastries using ingredients that were already on hand. The customers were eager to try her delightful additions. The pastries were light, scrumptious, and beautiful to look at. Lorenzo was impressed, and sales confirmed Sky's success. The extra demands added two more hours to Sky's workday. Although the time went by quickly, at the end of the day her energy was spent, and she was ready for bed.

Sky struggled to stay awake for Eric, but fell quickly to sleep, sometimes reading a book, sometime watching the evening news. Often, when she woke in the morning, she found Eric passed out on the chair in front of the TV. She would wake him and lead him to their bed, wondering how he was able to sleep sitting up in a chair.

It was Sky's day off and, as usual, when she awoke she found Eric asleep in front of the TV. Obviously intoxicated, she led him to bed ignoring his inaudible mumbling. He was in no shape to share the day with her, so she showered, dressed quietly, and left.

Anna and Bill were scheduled to arrive the following day. Although she was excited, Sky was not sure that Eric was going to be available before the ceremony to share Rome with her family. She was hoping he would carve out some time for them, and didn't want to have to explain his absence. She wrestled with his apparent indifference about the wedding plans, wondering if it was a man thing or if he just didn't care. Sky was afraid her parents would ask questions that she wasn't prepared to answer.

Eric worked long hours; she understood that. She worked long hours as well. In addition to her long workday, she took care of their apartment and was chief cook and bottle washer; additionally, she was paying most of their bills. Sky couldn't remember the last time Eric gave her money. He just bought a new motorcycle and was spending money every evening drinking and eating with his crew.

Eric said he loved her, and he wanted to spend the rest of his life with her, but that's not how he was acting. Nothing had changed since the night he asked her to marry him. He told her he'd settled into his job and would have more time for them, but that hadn't happened. Since their move to Rome, Sky had all of the responsibility, and he was doing whatever he wanted with his time and money. It was not how she imagined their life together, and it was not what he promised.

Sky didn't want to think anymore about how Eric had been acting. She needed to do something to make herself feel better. The wedding was planned, and her mother and Bill were on the way to Rome. Yet, she again doubted Eric and was not sure marrying him was what she wanted.

Out in the beautiful, May sunshine she felt better. A walk-through Villa Borghese, the largest park in Rome, was just what she needed. Taking her time to enjoy the sights always made her feel more connected to Rome. The park was dotted with museums, a theatre, a beautiful lake, and numerous fountains. It was one of her favorite places to take a stroll and clear her head. She loved the natural beauty, ancient architecture, and the buzz of visitors busily snapping pictures. Hikers and bikers of all ages were out enjoying the day. Sitting on a rock facing the water, Sky tried to relax and stop her downward spiraling self-doubt.

She assured herself that everything was going to be okay. Eric loved her. These doubts were because she was tired and a little stressed from putting the wedding together in such a short time. She breathed in the fresh air, enjoying the warmth of the sun on her face, as she continued on her walk.

The sound of wrestling leaves, in a cluster of shrubs rich with blooms, got her attention. She turned and looked more closely in their direction. From the corner of her eye she saw a little, golden furred creature moving quickly across her path. It disappeared into an opening between boulders shaded by pine trees. She was sure it was a coyote.

*    *    *    *    *

The next morning Sky was scheduled to work a half day. Eric had the day off. When she left for work he was in a deep sleep after another late night. The plan was to go to the airport later that evening to pick up her mother and Bill. When she arrived at work she busied herself, getting ready for the early morning breakfast crowd. Lorenzo peeked out of the storage room and waive hello as he always did.

At ten o'clock, he approached her and untied her apron. "You will go home now, and get ready for your wedding. I will take it from here. When you return you will be the Mrs. I think it suits you. Now go."

Sky was surprised by his kindness. She finished up and headed home to the apartment. Her heart was racing with all she had to do. They had until eight that night to tie up all the loose ends, and then they could relax and enjoy their wedding day. She was glad that Eric had the day off, she needed him to give her a hand with the last-minute details.

To Sky's surprise, when she arrived home the apartment door was not locked. She was certain she had locked it when she left for work that morning. Eric never got up this early, but she wondered if he had gone out for something, forgetting to lock the door behind him. Entering, she saw a jacket hanging over the kitchen chair and a pair of loafers at the foot of the disheveled bed. Sky knew they weren't Eric's. The bathroom door was open, and she could hear the shower running. As Sky moved closer to the bathroom she heard voices. One she didn't recognize, the other was Eric's. It was clear that Eric had company in the shower. Sky hesitated for a moment. Eric had been distant, but another woman never entered her mind. When she drew back the shower curtain, to her surprise, she saw Eric in an embrace with a young, dark haired man.

Sky stared in disbelief. She stepped back banging into the door, then turned and left. Feeling off balance, she grabbed for her backpack almost falling. Struggling with what she had just seen, Sky ran from the apartment. Slamming the door loudly behind her; when she got outside, she leaned against the building, doubled over, and threw up. Her stomach was churning as she gasped for breath. Her eyes burned from uncontrollable tears, and she could hear her father's voice, loud and clear.

It was the same warning she heard when she was a little girl before she fell into the pond. "Danger, Sky, danger!"

Eric, with just a towel wrapped around him, stepped out into the street calling her name.

He leaned against the building beside her and tried to take her hands in his. "I'm sorry. I didn't mean for this to happen. I'm so sorry."

She pulled away and turned her back, unable to look at him. Eric tried to wrap his arms around her.

Grinding her teeth, she shouted, "Don't touch me! How could you? You are a phony! You are a liar!"

Out of breath she walked away ignoring Eric's cries and pleas for forgiveness.

The airport was the only place she could think of to go. Returning to the apartment was not an option. The sight of Eric would make her sick. The other man was no one she knew. It didn't matter who he was. Now, it all made sense. He was using her, using their relationship as a facade. Her body ached from holding back the tears as she sat in the airport waiting for her family. How could she have been so naive? How was she going to tell her mother and Bill the sorted details? She and Eric were supposed to be married in two days. Everything had to be cancelled. It was her worst nightmare. Sky wondered how she could have been so stupid.

*    *    *    *    *

Anna and Bill knew something was wrong the minute they saw Sky at the airport.

Wrapping her arms around her daughter, Anna was the first to speak. "What is wrong? Where is Eric? Are you okay?"

As tears again filled her eyes, the only words Sky could say were, "The wedding is off."

Anna held her grieving daughter in silence as she sobbed. Sky's muffled, heartbroken sobbing brought tears to Anna's eyes and an ache to her heart. Bill pulled the luggage from the conveyer belt and moved everything close to the outer wall looking for privacy.

He was angry, but spoke softly. "Sky, how can we help?"

She looked up and closed her eyes. "I can't go back to the apartment right now. I hope he doesn't come to the hotel tonight. I don't want to talk to him."

Bill understood. "Let's get a cab. We'll go to the hotel and settle in for the night. If Eric wants to see you, I'll take care of him. He'll have to wait until you're ready."

Anna tried to sooth her daughter's pain. "We can talk about this when you're ready, Sky. Right now, you need a good night's sleep."

At the hotel, they went directly to the room reserved for them. Flipping the light switch they could see there were two double beds. They agreed the room would work for the night.

Anna tried to comfort Sky as best she could. "In the morning, when you are feeling better, you can tell us what is going on. Then we'll help you do whatever needs to be done."

Sky shook her head in agreement, put her backpack on the chair, pulled back the covers, and slipped into bed. Soft, muffled cries continued until she fell asleep. It was difficult for Anna and Bill to see their daughter in so much pain.

Bill took Anna's hand. "I'm angry, and I don't even know what's going on. I want to find Eric and beat the crap out of him."

Anna knew exactly how Bill was feeling. "Hopefully, in the morning, Sky will be able to talk about what's going on. Why don't we go to the dining room, have a glass of wine, and unwind? I don't know about you, but I'm still reeling from a suddenly planned wedding being cancelled, the long flight, and the time change. I don't think I'm ready to sleep yet. Are you?"

Bill was on board. They left a light on in the bathroom for Sky, locked the door, and headed for the hotel restaurant.

In the morning, a puffy-eyed Sky told them about the last couple of months - what Eric was saying, and what he was actually doing. Sky was trying not to make excuses for him. As they talked she knew she should be thankful that she found out about his lies before they were married. She couldn't help but wondered how long he had been cheating on her. Was he always interested in men? Did he have male boyfriends in college? She didn't see the signs. Her head was spinning with questions. How could she have let this happen? She was in mourning for the Eric she thought she knew and loved, but not quite sure who Eric really was.

Bill and Anna went back to the apartment with Sky the next morning to pack up her belongings. Eric opened the door, looking and smelling like he had been up all night drinking and smoking. There was no one else in the apartment.

Sky walked passed him. "I'm taking my things. I don't want anything else, just my clothes. I don't ever want to see you again."

Eric staggered slightly. "Sky, can't we talk about this? I - I love you. I'm a different person in Rome than I am at home. I can't explain it. My parents had expectations that I had to live up to. Maybe, if we move back to New Hampshire it will all be okay."

Sky shook her head. "You told me you loved me and wanted to marry me, have a family, and spend the rest of your life with me. All the while you were cheating on me. You can't even figure out what sex you want, never mind commit to a lifetime with me."

Bill placed his large hand on Eric's arm. "I think it would be better if you left while Sky puts her things together."

Anna remained silent as Eric walked passed her and left the apartment. Sky's anger reached a peak as she slammed drawers, emptied her bureau, and collected her personal items, crying all the while. As they left the space that had been her home - the space she had personally chosen and so loved - she knew she was closing the door forever. Bill hailed a cab, and they returned to the hotel with Sky and all of her belongings.

Anna took Sky's hand. "I know this is an awful day for you. Try to remember that you'll love again. Eric was not who you believed him to be. I'm not sure Eric knows who he is. Part of what happened was because of his deceit, but part of it was the illusion you created around him. You made excuses for his behavior. It may take time, but you'll meet someone who is everything they appear to be. I had true love twice in my life, once with your father before his accident and then with Bill. Not all men are like Eric, a trickster; I promise you."

Sky listened quietly to what her mother was saying and knew she was right but, at the moment, she didn't want to think about it. She was hurt, and angry, and felt that she never again wanted a man in her life.

Sky turned to Anna. "Do you think the coyote I saw was telling me that Eric was deceiving me? Is it possible that my father's spirit animal is now my spirit animal?"

Anna smiled. "I think that there are things in life that we don't fully understand. Think about it, and you decide if you think it's possible."

*　　　*　　　*　　　*　　　*

Sky didn't want to think anymore. She was tired of thinking. After canceling the reservations she made for the wedding, she packed her wedding gown and shoes and gave them to her mother to take back to New Hampshire. They had one more day in Rome together, and Sky wanted to share the things of Rome that made her happy, and not think about the person that made her sad.

It took all of her strength to think about something other than her cheating boyfriend and cancelled wedding. Keeping busy was her solution. Her mother and Bill wanted to see where she worked and meet the people she worked with. Their first stop was the café. Lorenzo was surprised to see her, but greeted them warmly. He quickly served them a cappuccino and one of Sky's special desserts. The place was buzzing with customers, but Lorenzo took his time and told Anna and Bill how much he appreciated Sky's talent and how valuable she was to his business.

He took her hand and looked into her eyes. "Sky, I wish for you a long, happy marriage. It is in my best interest that you stay with us for a very long time."

Although a little uncomfortable, they all laughed at his joke and didn't mention that the wedding had been called off.

Bill broke the awkward silence. "I'm so glad we met you, Lorenzo. It makes me feel good that our girl is happy where she's working. It's good to know that she's appreciated."

As they finished their cappuccino Sky told them the history of their next stop, the Coliseum. She could not let them go home without seeing the amazing wonder. It was one of her favorites.

Turning to leave they saw Lorenzo making his way through the crowded dining area. "Sky, keep your ears open. My sister, Rosa, is moving, and I'm looking for a tenant for the studio above the café. I'd like to put someone in there that I can trust. So, if you know of anyone, please tell them to give me a call."

Sky shook her head and smiled. "As a matter of fact, I have someone in mind, Lorenzo. I'll talk to you when I get back to work. Is that okay?"

Surprised, but obviously pleased, Lorenzo agreed. "I wasn't expecting to find someone so quickly. Good. Good, we'll talk when you get back."

When they got outside Anna immediately questioned Sky. "Are you thinking about taking the studio for yourself?"

Tears again filled her eyes. "I guess I am. I can't live with Eric. I don't want to go back to the apartment we shared, and I'm not ready to go home. I really love my job, and I don't want to leave it. It's just what I've been waiting for. I need a few more days before talking to Lorenzo about it but, yes, I think living above the café would work."

Bill and Anna assumed Sky was coming home with them. They were surprised and unhappy that she was thinking about staying.

Anna, however, was not sure Sky was ready to make any decisions after all she had been through. "Why don't we just enjoy the day. Jumping into decisions after the emotional turmoil you've been in doesn't make sense. Take a deep breath. Today, show us around Rome, and we can discuss this later on tonight."

They agreed they wouldn't talk about Eric or the cancelled wedding. Instead, they would fill the last day they had together in Rome with happy memories, and there was so much Sky wanted them to see. She wanted to share all the beauty and art that was around them. Her heart was heavy, but she so loved Rome. Sky wanted Bill and her mother to see it the way she did, hoping they would understand why she wasn't ready to leave.

The day flew by. Bill and Anna were completely captivated by the wonders of Rome. They depended on the transit system to move from one location to another throughout the day. The weather was perfect and, when they weren't marveling at the old-world architecture, the neighborhood markets captured their attention.

That evening, after several messages from Eric, Sky turned her cell phone off. Bill and Anna made reservations for dinner in the hotel restaurant. Sky, although not hungry, knew their time together was coming to an end, and agreed to join them.

At dinner Bill was adamant. "Now, Sky, we cannot leave you in Rome by yourself. Come home and find a job in the States. You have experience and talent. It shouldn't take long for a restaurant or hotel to recognize your value and hire you. I would feel much better if you came home with us tomorrow."

Anna agreed with Bill. "I know you've been through a lot. Making decisions when you're upset isn't a good idea. Rome is beautiful, but it's not your home."

Sky said she would think about returning home. She was too tired to argue and just wanted to go to bed. They toasted to new beginnings for Sky, finished their meal, and went back to the hotel room.

*        *        *        *        *

The next morning Anna and Bill let Sky sleep. When she awoke they were packed and ready to go to the airport.

Anna offered Sky a cup of cappuccino. "Okay, honey, why don't you get dressed. We have to get a cab and head to the airport. All of your things are ready to go."

Sky took a sip, savoring the deep flavor for a moment. "Mom, Dad, I've decided to stay. I know you want me to come home. I understand and love that you want to protect me. I'm twenty-five years old, and I've been living in Rome for almost three years now. I'm comfortable and very happy with my job. The biggest problem I had was Eric. He is no longer in my life. I've decided to talk to Lorenzo about the studio apartment above the café. I was in it once when his sister lived there, and it's perfect for me. It's small, but not any smaller than the apartment I was sharing with Eric. It's convenient and, I think you can tell, Lorenzo is a good friend and will be nearby. It feels like a good fit."

Anna was disappointed, but not surprised. "I was afraid that's what you were going to say. You're right, you're not a child. We want to protect you from anything and anyone that would hurt you. We couldn't protect you from Eric, but we know this is your decision. I think you know you can come home at any time. We love you."

Bill was not happy about her decision, but agreed. Her plan was to stay in hotel room for two more days. After Bill and her mother left for home she would go to the café and speak to Lorenzo. She wasn't completely sure about her decision but, at least for a while, she would live life by herself, something she had never done before. Now, it was just her.

The goodbyes were difficult. They didn't know when they would see each other again. Sky assured her mother and Bill she would let them know about everything that was happening in her life and, of course, there was Skype.

After she left the airport Sky headed for the café to speak to Lorenzo. She wasn't sure how much she would tell him about her broken engagement and canceled wedding, but she knew she wanted the apartment. Lorenzo listened patiently to every detail of her upcoming wedding, now she was going to tell him about the breakup. What would he think of her?

*    *    *    *    *

Sky guessed that Lorenzo was about 10 years older than she was. His father was the original owner of the café and, when he retired, Lorenzo took over adding his own unique flair. He was a hard worker and very kind to his employees. Working in the kitchen since he was eleven, he knew what the customers wanted, peak sales times, and how to manage his employees. It all seemed so natural for him. Sky wanted to develop his kind of skill. She knew about the mechanics of her craft and was a bit of an artist, but what she wanted now was the experience and instincts that Lorenzo had. She wanted to be extraordinary.

Sky didn't know much about Lorenzo except for the story of the café that was printed on the menu and a few stories told by coworkers about the family owned vineyard. Lorenzo spent two days a week there. The wine produced at the vineyard was exceptional and won many prestigious awards. The café was the only place in Rome the label could be found, and sales were quite impressive.

Lorenzo was private about his personal life and rarely spoke about his family, unlike Sky who talked openly about her family, friends, and college days. Except for a couple of long-term employees, most of the help at the restaurant were transients, college students, or travelers staying short term while getting to know the countryside.

Everyone knew about the family business and how it grew and was passed down from father to son, but there was little known about the family's personal lives. Sky didn't know where Lorenzo lived, only that his sister lived above the café for several years. She too was private and rarely spoke about family. Lorenzo was at the restaurant from sunup to sundown and, other than his trips to the vineyard, he didn't seem to have much of a life outside of the café.

Lorenzo was surprised to see Sky. "What are you doing here? Shouldn't you be on your honeymoon?"

Sky grinned. "Oh, about that, I called it off."

Lorenzo looked puzzled. "I'm sorry. I think I'm sorry. Should I be sorry? Are you okay?"

Sky and he sat down at a small, round, multicolored, mosaic table in the restaurant's kitchen. She told him that she and Eric wanted different things in life. They had grown apart, and she was glad they realized it before they married. He listened quietly and expressed his sympathy.

Quickly she changed the subject. "I'm interested in the studio apartment that your sister, Rosa, is leaving. How soon will it be available? Is it furnished, and how much do you want monthly?"

Lorenzo thought for a moment. "She moved this weekend. Rosa took a job in Tuscany and begins work on Monday. I'm happy for her, it's a good fit. Let's see now. Yes, it is furnished, and you can move in right away if you would like. I'll give you the first month at no charge, just so you can get yourself settled. After all, you are like family."

Sky was happy and relieved that she had a place to live. It wasn't a big deal for her to move in. Other than her clothing she had very few belongings. Lorenzo offered to help her, but she really didn't need his help and wanted to settle in by herself. This was a new chapter in her life.

Sky sent a text to Anna and Bill telling them she took the apartment over the café, and that she was able to move in right away. She felt it would help them feel better about her decision.

Eric's attempts to contact her dwindled and finally stopped. As the weeks passed Sky was feeling her decision to stay was a good one. She escaped into her work. On days off she walked one of the many busy marketplaces or explored a new neighborhood trattoria. She was pleased with herself. Her Italian was improving, and she was happy with her new living space. As she added decorative pieces she bought while wandering the outdoor markets, the apartment was feeling more like her own. One of her favorite market finds was a small, ceramic coyote that reminded her that her father was watching over her. She was sure, now, that the coyote showed up in her life to warn her that she was off track. Thinking of the little golden coyote made her smile and feel connected to her father.

*    *    *    *    *

Mornings were always hectic at the café. Sky was able to balance the changing menu and the demand for constant favorites with ease. She and Lorenzo developed a kind of shorthand between them that required few words. They were on the same track when it came to maintaining excellence. After a long day Sky retreated upstairs to her flat for a soak in the tub, and indulged in slices of cheese, a croissant, and a glass of wine before going to bed. Life was hectic, but full. The sadness she felt over the end of her relationship with Eric faded. The American gals that she had so much in common with became her family away from home. There was little time for anything else. Café workers came and went making her a senior employee in her third year.

One evening after work, as she was getting ready to leave, unexpectedly, Lorenzo asked if she would like to join him in a glass of wine. Although she was tired and was looking forward to a long soak in the tub, she accepted his invitation. Lorenzo popped the cork and poured them each a glass of dark, red wine. It was unusual, but she was intrigued. Sky sat down wondering what it was all about.

Lorenzo extended his hand in a grand gesture, offering her the wine glass. "You have come a long way from the girl I interviewed three years ago. In my humble opinion, you have become a master pastry chef in a very short time. I want you to know that I believe you are adding a wonderful dimension to the café. It is my pleasure to increase your salary. You certainly are worth more money."

Sky was pleasantly surprised at the substantial increase in pay. "Thank you, Lorenzo. I didn't expect this, but I'm grateful. After Eric and I broke up I needed to focus on something other than all that had gone wrong in my life. You gave me the space to grow and feel good about what I was doing, and I really appreciate it."

After another glass of wine Sky knew it was time for her to climb the stairs and slip into the tub. Lorenzo filled her glass one more time. Because she had the following day off, she gave herself permission stay a little longer. A relaxed visit with Lorenzo was a welcomed change from her constant running.

Lorenzo smiled and lifted his glass. "We work side by side every day creating pleasure for the palette. Let's drink to the continuation of a surprisingly successful team."

Sky liked the sound of that and repeated it. "Yes, a surprisingly successful team." She, again, lifted her glass and slowly sipped the wine, enjoying its rich bouquet.

Standing to leave, and sounding a little formal, she thanked Lorenzo. "You are a kind man. I appreciate that you've given me room to grow, and for your support during a time that was so difficult for me. I agree, we are a really good team."

She chuckled at herself and stepped slightly too far to the right almost losing her balance. Straightening quickly, she headed toward the door that lead upstairs to her apartment.

Lorenzo followed, neither of them saying a word. Sky opened the door to her flat and he followed her inside. When she turned toward him to speak, he pressed his finger to her lips stopping her. Taking a deep breath, she closed her eyes. Sky knew she had too much wine, but didn't care. She felt good. It all felt good.

Lorenzo moved closer wrapping his strong arms around her waist. He smelled of pastry and wine. As their lips met Sky's body relaxed into his. Slowly his hands moved from her waist, gliding gently upward along her back to her neck. He freed her dark curls from the tight knot that held her long, silky hair neatly in place. His lips, slightly moist, slid across her neck. Sky felt breathless as his warm tongue fluttered across her shoulder and moved to her breasts. Lorenzo's hands drifted across her hips as he tucked his fingers beneath her camisole, lifting it gently over her head. Sky had no desire to stop him, and was hungry for more.

As if her body was driven by a foreign energy, Sky accepted every pleasure Lorenzo offered. Responding to her awakened desires, Sky freed herself of all the constraints of the past. She enjoyed her surprising ability to accept and return unbridled passion.

Her tongue eagerly tasted the front of his neck as she savored his salty sweetness. Slowly unbuttoning his shirt, her senses were treated to his firm, sculptured chest. Sky's body stirred with a passion she had never experienced before. Lorenzo was a master who unlocked the symphony that was Sky, waiting to be played.

He gently laid her on the bed and they connected in a rhythmic embrace that released all they had to give. When Sky awoke the next morning, Lorenzo was gone.

Feeling slightly hung over, sky drew a bath and slipped into the tub, allowing her body to relax into the hot, lavender scented water. Thinking about the evening made her smile, but she wasn't sure what it was about. Was it the wine, the complements, or maybe the raise? It was, for her, raw, passionate, and delicious. She had been feeling less than attractive since Eric chose a man over her. It was a wonderful night, like nothing she had ever experienced before. He wanted her, and she hadn't felt desirable in a very long time. Sky felt unleashed, satisfied and more aware of the gifts her sexuality had to offer.

*     *     *     *     *

Sky was happy she had the day off. There was nothing she wanted to do and little she had to do. The sun was bright, and the view from her window invited her to go outside and enjoy the day. By the time Sky dressed and was ready to go, customers were already arriving at the café. She glanced inside and saw Lorenzo busily working behind the counter smiling graciously. He spoke to each customer as if they were family. Sky felt a little giddy seeing him. A quick, unacknowledged waived made her feel like a little girl with a crush. So much had changed for her in just one night. Wondering if she was making the night more important than it was, she walked to the neighborhood trattoria and sipped a cappuccino to clear her head.

The next day at work was awkward for Sky. She wasn't sure how to act around Lorenzo. They had made love, but she wasn't sure how she was feeling about it. As the day unfolded they were no different, just their usual interactions; friendly, work related conversations. She was glad she was busy. Sky worked hard to put their night together out of her thoughts. The long day finally ended, and it was time for her to go upstairs. As she hung her apron in the back room, Lorenzo peeked out of the kitchen.

He held up a bottle of red wine. "Good job today, Sky. Are you interested in toasting to the end of another good day with me?"

The giddiness returned and her body flushed warm and tingly, overflowing into a "Yes, joining you in a toast to a good day will make for the end of a perfect day."

After a glass of wine, they retired to Sky's flat and lost themselves again in each other bodies. Sky floated to sleep with Lorenzo's arms wrapped around her but, again, when she awoke in the morning he was gone.

As she readied for work she looked in the mirror and could see that the ecstasy of the evening left a visible glow on her skin. She asked herself what was happening. Could she accept the friendly but distant work relationship during the day that turned into passionate lovemaking at night? Should she give it some time? Could it change into the kind of relationship her mother and Bill had? That's what she really wanted. That's what she thought she had with Eric. Sky didn't know what Lorenzo wanted or what he was looking for.

The polite and friendly daytime relationship continued as did their passion in the evenings. Lorenzo was gone every morning. Sky had no idea how long he stayed, but she knew he held her tenderly until she fell asleep. She stopped questioning herself about where the relationship was going and simply enjoyed their evenings together and her newly awakened passion.

*    *    *    *    *

A phone call with her mother put Sky in a nostalgic frame of mind as she remembered how Bill stepped in taking the place of the father she never knew. He was gentle and kind to both of them. He showed up to give them whatever was needed and never looked for anything in return. Sky watched as her mother and Bill grew closer and their love blossomed. That was the kind of relationship she wanted. Just talking to Bill and hearing the concern in his voice made her miss him. How lucky her mother had been to meet two men in her life that she could love and be loved in return. Sky thought she had that kind of love with Eric, but the time was short lived and turned out to be only a façade for him. It was time for her to talk to her mother.

Sunday evening Sky and Anna finally connected. Sky kept her voice light and playful. "Hey, Mom, I have a question for you. When you fell in love with Dad, and then Bill, how did you know they were the one? Did you know what you were looking for? How long was it before you were sure?"

Anna was suspicious. "Wow, Sky, do you have someone in mind?"

Sky laughed at her mother's question feeling a little uncomfortable. "Not really. I have finally gotten Eric out of my mind and heart, and I think I'm ready for a relationship, but I don't want to do the same thing again. You know, I don't want to see things that aren't there, or make up stories about their character instead of seeing who they really are."

Anna was happy her daughter trusted her enough to ask the really hard questions she was asking. "Yes, Sky, I know what you mean. I'm glad you're ready to fall in love again. Half the battle is being open to it. Read the letter your father left for you. I think his message is a loving one, and one that you can think about when you meet someone new that you are drawn to."

Sky had forgotten about the letter. After saying goodbye, she went to her little, wooden treasure chest, opened it, and read the letter out loud. As she did, she felt as if her father was there with her, and she could feel his love and concern for her. There had always been a place in her heart that ached to know him. This letter was the closest connection she would ever have.

Sky thought about Lorenzo. He listened to her every word and asked for nothing in return – except for their evening nightcap. He made her happy and awakened a hunger she never knew she had. Although Sky didn't think she was ready for more, there was an aching inside that was asking to be soothed.

*     *     *     *     *

Many calls from home went unanswered. After excitedly telling her mother and father about her raise in pay, and asking her mother a few questions, there was very little else Sky wanted to talk about. She didn't know what to say about her relationship with Lorenzo. It was enjoyable, but it was more like a bedtime story than a lifetime story. Sky and Lorenzo talked about work, recipes, creative license, and the wonder of Rome. They were friends, work mates, and enjoyed wonderful sex - sex like she had never known before. There was no talk of love or the future. Her mother and Bill would ask questions that she wasn't ready to answer and she was sure they wouldn't approve. On the occasions when Sky called home the conversation was casual. Her message was always that she was fine, and they didn't have to worry.

Months passed since Sky and Lorenzo first made love. There was still work Lorenzo and bedroom Lorenzo. She tried not to think about it, but was struggling with the distinct differences between the bedroom relationship and the work relationship. In time, Sky stopped wondering what her mother and Bill would say, because she knew.

One evening after love making, as he held her, Sky ventured into untraveled territory. "Lorenzo, what do you do on your day off? Where do you go?"

Sky had often wondered. Asking the longtime workers casually about where they believed he spent his time off, the only answer she got was that he went to the vineyard.

Lorenzo never talked about himself unless he was asked a question. "I inherited my father's vineyard. When I'm there, I have dinner with the family and I work to keep everything in order. The Vino Roma wine label is mine. The vineyard has been in my family for four generations."

Sky imagined Lorenzo working the land. The wine his family's vineyard produced was wonderful, and she was sure it took a lot of commitment to produce such a delicate vintage.

Still wanting to hear more about his personal life, she pressed on. "I would love to see the vineyard."

Lorenzo kissed her lips and slipped out of bed disappearing into the bathroom. When he returned he was passionate and tender, and they made love until early morning.

When Sky opened her eyes with the rising sun, as always, she was alone. Still floating on the evening's intense, physical connection, Sky lingered in bed. The question she was asking herself was why she needed more than what they had.

When she arose she made her bed, poured herself a cup of cappuccino, and got ready for work. Grabbing her bag to leave, she brushed against the end table and knocked her little, ceramic coyote to the floor. Sky watched in horror as it fell and shattered into pieces. She stepped back against the wall, staring in disbelief.

The symbol of her father's spirit guide was destroyed. Tears rose, flooded her eyes, and rolled down her cheeks. She wiped them away quickly pretending they didn't exist. Clearly it was a sign that she was on the wrong path; something she had been feeling for several months. Denial would no longer work. It was time for her to be honest with herself about her relationship with Lorenzo.

Sky decided it was time for her to have a serious talk with him. She wondered why he hadn't invited her to his family vineyard. She wanted to know if their relationship was just about the sex. It was suddenly important for her to find out what she meant to him.

Sky went about her workday only half engaged in what she was doing, waiting for Lorenzo to appear. She looked up when she heard a commotion at the front of the café. Lorenzo entered holding the hands of two little girls. They looked to be eight and nine years old, and were wearing parochial school uniforms. Both had their long, black hair pulled back tightly into a ponytail. Lorenzo, seeing Sky, walked toward her, leading the girls who followed him hesitantly.

When they stopped, Lorenzo dropped their hands and gestured to Sky. "I would like to introduce you to my daughters, Teresa, and Catherine. Girls, say hello to Sky. She is our pastry chef, and a very good one at that."

The girls gave a little wave and ducked quickly behind their father.

Then he waived in the direction of an attractive young woman.

Moving through the cluster of customers she made her way to his side and slipped her arm around his. "Oh, yes, Sky, this is my wife, Sofia."

Sky went numb. She worked to digest what he just said. A quick assessment of what she was seeing and she understood. The girls looked exactly like Lorenzo, and his wife was quite beautiful. He was letting her know exactly where their relationship stood.

Lorenzo's wife extended her hand to Sky.

In a melodious, Italian accent she greeted her with a friendly smile. "It is nice to meet you, Sky, I have heard so much about you."

Sophia then took the girls' hands, turned, and led them to the door.

Looking back, she threw a kiss with a wave of her hand. "We have to go now. Lorenzo, we'll see you this weekend? Sky, it was nice to finally meet you. Ciao."

Lorenzo smiled. "Yes. Yes, see you this weekend. Love you girls."

Sky searched Lorenzo's face for – she didn't know what - but he turned and went into the kitchen without a word. Sky was in shock. Lorenzo was married and had children. Why had he not told her? The bigger question was why she hadn't asked.

Sky made it through the day avoiding Lorenzo as much as possible. She just wanted to finish her work and leave. When her day was done she quickly left for her flat. Closing the door behind her she saw her coyote figurine in pieces strewn across the floor. Now, she, too, was in pieces.

There came a knock on the door. Sky prayed it was not Lorenzo. As she opened it her heart raced. There he stood holding a bottle of wine and two glasses.

With a smile she knew only too well, he said, "Sky, you left too soon. We haven't had our end of day glass of wine. We have it now. Yes?"

Sky stepped back. "I - I didn't know you were married. You never told me. Why didn't you tell me?"

Lorenzo smiled a crooked smile. "You didn't ask. Our love making is good, is it not? I go home to the vineyard, to my wife and children, two nights a week. That's how we live. I give them everything they want and need. It's all good. Why are you upset with me?"

Putting her hand against his chest, Sky pushed him back into the hallway and shut the door. "I'm upset with you because it's not okay! It is not okay to me!"

Sky cried herself to sleep and, in the morning, called home. "Mom, I would like to come home, please. I don't think I want to live here anymore."

Anna was surprised, but was happy to send her a ticket home. Bill was grateful that she was finally coming to her senses. He was sure she had a better future at home where her family and friends were.

*　　*　　*　　*　　*

On the flight back, Sky slept. Her return trip was very different from the trip she took years earlier. She and Eric were headed to Rome with dreams of a beautiful life together. It was just that, a dream. It was not real. The relationship for Eric was only pretence. It was an acceptable story for his mother's and father's benefit. When she discovered the truth, she blamed herself for being so naive. He was not the person he pretended to be. Sky forgave him, but she could not forgive herself for not knowing - for not paying attention to the signs.

Lorenzo was wonderful and awful. Sky couldn't say for sure if she was in love with him. She knew she loved how he made her feel. She wanted him. What she didn't want was another woman's husband. He, too, deceived her, but she hadn't asked the questions. Both relationships ended painfully. Sky thought Lorenzo was someone she could count on, and she was right. She could count on him to be her boss and her lover but, the reality was, he was no more real than Eric had been. She had to accept responsibility for her poor choices. It was about her wanting and needing to be in love. She had fallen for two tricksters, and it would be a long time before she could trust herself with love again.

Sky was grateful that during the years she lived in Rome she was able to experience all of its magnificence. Before she left for the airport to head back to the White Mountains of New Hampshire, she once again visited the Trevi Fountain and threw a coin in, hopping to ensure that there was a place in time that she would return.

*     *     *     *     *

Anna and Bill meet her at Logan Airport. The three-hour drive home was filled with polite conversation. Sky carefully crafted a story of changes that occurred at the café. She and Lorenzo didn't see eye to eye, and she decided that it was time to make a move back to the States. They were still friends, and she was grateful for all he taught her. That was her story, and it was all she wanted them to know.

At the house, the boys greeted her with kisses and cries of welcome. Her room was just as she had left it. Sitting on her bed she looked around. All the pictures on the walls were exactly as they were when she moved away. The lamp she picked out when she was a senior in high school sat on her end table, and the big calendar still hung on her closet door with all the little notes written in the date squares. The month she left home for Rome was still the one displayed. All of these things were so important to her when she was young. Even the smell of her room made her feel happy and hopeful.

Sky placed the little box that her father made for her on the table beside her bed. It was returning home as well.

Opening it, she read her father's letter out loud. "For my beautiful, Sky. I made this treasure box with love in my heart for you. Every grain, every curve, every nuance is fashioned with my love for you in mind. Just as the merging of these woods created an extraordinary blend of strength and softness, life will ask you to do the same. As you grow, at times you will be called on to stand strong and fight hard for what you believe in. Love will require that you hold softness in your heart. There is a beauty in the mix. When real love enters your life, you will recognize the blending. The mix will be familiar, a perfect fit. Never let it go. Love forever, Daddy."

Sky knew now, as never before, how true his words were. It made her feel close to him. She liked what it said, and she vowed that she would never again lose track of her own needs. Her father's message was about true love; the blending of the wants and needs of two people, not a surrender of one to complete the life goals of the other.

\*     \*     \*     \*     \*

Sky's next step was to find a job. The years she worked at the café in Rome gave her confidence. She knew she had the skills necessary to handle any job she wanted. Living in a resort area with many restaurants and hotels would, no doubt, offer many opportunities for a job in her field. After networking with a few college friends in the area, she lined up several interviews. Living at home allowed her to be selective. It was important to her that the job she accepted be multifaceted and offer her an environment in which she could continue to learn and grow, display her craft, and excel in her field.

After two months of disappointing interviews Sky was beginning to be concerned. The people she interviewed with were impressed with her experience in Rome, but the positions did not offer her the opportunity to do what she was really interested in, developing her mastery in pastry artistry.

There was one more interview scheduled. It was with the chef at the Mount Washington Hotel in Bretton Woods, and it was the most interesting and exciting of them all. Sky loved the Spanish Renaissance architecture of the hotel and was captured by its history. The resort was a historic site dating back to 1902. The elegant, luxury hotel offered decadent dining, exactly what she was looking for.

The interview couldn't have gone better. The chef spent time in Rome and was a fan of Café Roma. It wasn't long before the phone call came offering her the position as head pastry chef. He wanted her to start as soon as possible. Anna and Bill couldn't be happier for her. They were considering postponing their travel plans until Sky found the job she was looking for, worried that she might have to look out of state. Now, everything was falling into place and life was unfolding for Sky just as they had hoped. Even the boys seemed peppier.

Bill was preparing to retire from the Forestry Service after thirty years of dedication. He and Anna had vacationed abroad over the years, but seeing all the beauty and wonder of the United States, including all the National Forests, was what they wanted to do now. Their new RV was in the driveway waiting for their sightseeing adventure to begin. Now that Sky was home, she and the boys would have the house to themselves while Bill and Anna traveled cross country.

Sky was happy, too. It was a very exciting time in her life. On her return flight from Rome she didn't think she would ever be happy again. Now she was home and was about to begin her dream job. She had a few days to herself before starting the next phase of her career.

*     *     *     *     *

There were so many memories for her in the old house. Although she had to leave the excitement of Rome, it was time to end that chapter of her life. Sky was happy to once again be living in New Hampshire. It was home, and it was where she was the happiest. Once winter came she would ski again for the first time in many years. When she was chasing her career and accommodating Eric's dreams, she didn't have the time or the money to do the things she loved. Now she would once again enjoy skiing the trails of New Hampshire.

Almost finished with her unpacking, Sky returned her treasure box to the table beside her bed where it had been when she was a girl. Her Dad's note was tucked neatly inside.

The sun was setting, and Sky was thinking about supper. Her mother and Bill would be home soon, and she wanted to surprise them with a gourmet meal. First, she was going to feed the boys and let them out for a run.

Looking into the refrigerator she decided she would have to go grocery shopping if she was going to prepare the meal she had in mind. Sky hadn't been shopping in the local market for years. Laughing to herself, she imagined seeing some of the same faces she left behind when she headed to Rome. It was, after all, a very close-knit community, and things didn't change very often.

The boys, barking, moved toward the front door letting Sky know someone was approaching. Opening the door, her guardians took their place beside her, sizing up the visitor. There stood a tall, trim, very attractive man, who she guessed was in his early thirties. His eyes were dark blue, the same blue as the sky that evening. His light hair peeked out in curls from under his ball cap.

"Can I help you?" she asked.

"Hi, my name is Gavin - Gavin Holden. I'm looking for Aaron - Aaron Rogers. Does he still live here?"

Sky tilted her head and asked, "Why are you looking for him?"

"It's a long story. I was a kid when we met. We were in the hospital at the same time. I've just moved back to the area and was thinking about him. I thought I'd stop by to see how he was doing. It's been quite a few years. After he was released from the hospital he came back to see me before I went home, just as he promised."

Sky was speaking to a friend of her father's. He was only a few years older than she was, and had more of a relationship with her father than she did. She wanted to know more.

Stepping aside, Sky asked him to come in. "Please have a seat."

The boys circled around him as he moved to the couch. Sitting, he leaned over and let each of the boys sniff his hand. Then he patted each one's head and stroked their backs as he spoke. Sky could see he passed the dog test and she agreed with their approval.

Sky sat down stiffly in the chair across from him. "Aaron was my father. He passed away twenty years ago in an accident on the mountain."

Obviously saddened, Gavin lowered his head. "I'm so sorry. I didn't know. The last time I saw him must have been just before the accident. It was a long time ago, but I was in the area and thought it wouldn't hurt to see if he was still around."

The handsome stranger shared his story with Sky. He told her that when he was ten he was in the hospital being treated for acute lymphoblastic leukemia. The chemo treatments left him skinny, pale, and bald. His mother and father lived two hours away and had to work every day to pay the mounting medical bills. They came after work, stayed for an hour, and took the long drive home again. Often, when the weather was bad, they would call him and visit by phone. He was sick, alone, and lonely most of the time.

Aaron came to his room daily. In his wheelchair, he sat by Gavin's bed and told him stories of the White Mountains and the Indian tribes that at one time inhabited them.

Gavin stared out the window. "Your father knew so much about the forest; the fir, hemlock, and Juniper trees, and all the plants and shrubs native to the area. He described for me how each tree and plant added its own touch of color in autumn, and he painted a picture with words that still linger in my memory. To this day it fuels my longing for the White Mountains in the fall. Aaron, your father, told me stories I could get lost in, stories that took me away from the hospital bed that was my home for so long. I imagined each trail as he described it to me. He gave me hope that some day I would be well enough to hike the trails and mountainside."

"We played a game. We would see who could name the most animals that we might meet on a trail in the mountains. We made up stories, and made goofy sounds, imitating what we thought each creature's voice might sound like if they could talk. He told me about his Vision Quest when he was fifteen, how the coyote visited him, and how he knew it was his totem animal. He was patient and answered all my questions, explaining all that his totem animal meant."

"Your father warned me that I might meet a wild animal while on a trail, and told me what I needed to do to stay safe while I was hiking."

Sky was in awe of the story and the handsome stranger that was telling it. "I wish he could have told me those stories."

Gavin looked puzzled. "Is this making you sad? I'll go now. I'm sorry if I've made you uncomfortable."

Sky reached out and touched the stranger's arm. "Please continue. I'm sad because I never got to know my father. You are helping me put some of the missing pieces together. Please go on."

Gavin continued telling the stories of his time with Aaron so many years ago. "I remember the day he went home from the hospital. He came to my room to say goodbye and promised he would be back to celebrate the day I was well enough to go home. I missed him when he left and was very lonely when his visits stopped."

Gavin remembered that Aaron used a cane and looked stronger when he paid him the last visit as he promised. The visit was bitter sweet. Gavin was in full remission and was going home, but this was their final goodbye.

Gavin lifted his chin as if Aaron was standing in front of him. "On that visit, he brought me a beautiful, wooden box that he made for me. He called it a treasure box. It was made from ash and white cedar. It was magnificent. He told me he hand-polished it. Aaron, your father, said to remember that one of the treasures the box held for me was the spirit of my one, true love. When I was ready, I would find her. Of course, I was ten at the time, and my one true love didn't really seem important."

Finishing his story Gavin stood to leave. "I'm sorry to hear your dad is no longer with us. He was a great comfort and inspiration to me when I really needed it. I'll always be grateful that he came into my life when he did. I spent a lot of time in that hospital room alone. Your dad gave me hope, an escape, and something to look forward to. I will never forget him."

Sky stood. "Wait."

She left the room and hurried up the stairs, returning with her little treasure box for Gavin to see.

Handing it to him she asked, "Is this like the one my dad gave to you?"

Turning it ever so slowly he said, "Yes, it's exactly the same, only smaller. In fact, I think this would fit perfectly inside the one your father made for me. It's as if they are two pieces of the same beautiful puzzle."

Sky was holding back tears. "He made this for me, but no one knew about it until after the accident - after he died. It was in his workshop in the barn with a note."

She opened the box and handed the letter to Gavin to read. He spoke the last sentences out loud. "When real love enters your life, you will recognize the blending. The mix will be familiar, a perfect fit. Never let it go. Love forever, Daddy."

Gavin smiled broadly. He carefully returned the letter to the little box and placed it in her hands.

Getting ready to leave, he glanced at Sky. "I - I would really like to talk to you more about your dad. Do you think we could get together and have lunch, or dinner, or something sometime?"

"I think I would like that," Sky said beaming.

She watched him leave and noticed that her heart was beating a little faster. Standing in the doorway until she could no longer see his car, to her surprise, a little, golden coyote scurried into the driveway, stopped for a few seconds, and continued on its way.

Sky lifted her eyes to heaven. "Thank you, Daddy. I understand. Love you, too."